I0451897

HALLOWEEN BITES

13 SNACK-SIZED STORIES

2022

FROM BLACK MARE BOOKS

Halloween Bites 2022: 13 Snack-Sized Stories

© 2022 by Black Mare Books. All rights reserved.

Black Mare Books

First Edition 2022

ISBN: 978-1-959008-27-9

Contents

Welfare Check

By A.B. Richards

Mommy? Why is Mr. Gonzales out there with two policemen?"

Kinsey Lang peered through the front window at her landlord, who waved his hands around as he spoke to a couple of cops.

He always was excitable.

Kinsey forced a smile. "I have no idea, Joanna," she lied to the nine-year-old. "Take your brother and go to your rooms, okay? It'll be all right. Don't worry." She awkwardly used her left hand to tuck a lock of hair behind her daughter's ear that had stubbornly stuck to the girl's forehead.

"C'mon, Charlie. You heard what Mommy said."

The six-year-old stood, turning his head so he could use his one good eye to navigate. Kinsey watched until they disappeared into the hallway. She sighed and moved a chair against the wall to hide a hole in the sheetrock. The security deposit had been forfeited a long time ago, but she was still embarrassed for Mr. Gonzales to see the damage.

Would he blame her, like Randy always did?

Her husband had sworn it would be different this time. Guess he skipped the rent.

Again.

She knew exactly where it had gone. He'd stumbled in at six this morning reeking of cheap alcohol and cheaper perfume.

Kinsey took another look out the window. Neither officer had any paperwork. When they'd been evicted before, cops had handed her a whole stack of papers. But then again, she hadn't expected to see any.

This time.

She moved away from the glass and paced around the living room.

Last month she'd scraped together enough money to pay most of the rent from her assistance check and some cash Randy had hidden in the closet. It was Tuesday—her check had come in the mail today. Always sent to her mother's house, so Randy couldn't get at it. She'd called to say it arrived.

They had a code.

Hey, Kinsey. Big sale at Walmart. You wanna go?

Sure, Mama.

I'll come pick you up.

Because the one thing that Randy hated worse than being sober was going shopping, and food had to get into the house somehow. So he let her out, on a short, tight leash, holding the children hostage to make sure she returned.

Did they realize what was happening?

Even the cheapest level of store-brand cookie is still a cookie. Maybe that Mommy always came home with treats when she went shopping was all they needed to know. Safer that way.

He hadn't always been like that. Or perhaps that was just one of the lies she told when she asked herself why she didn't leave him. There were also practical considerations.

He said he'd kill her if she left him.

She had nowhere to go, anyway. Her stepfather hated children in general, and hated her specifically, so her mother was afraid to take her in. It would be hellish there, anyway.

Her father? He would have skinned Randy alive. If he hadn't died of a heart attack when the children were small.

The voices outside got closer. She desperately wanted Mr. Gonzales to stay outside. She wouldn't be able to bear the look on his face when he stepped inside and looked around.

She frowned as she almost tripped over her husband's out-stretched leg.

He even managed to miss the couch. Kinsey wrinkled her nose. He reeked of more than booze now. *Probably just as well. Easier to clean the tile than the upholstery.*

Mr. Gonzales and the officers were on the porch now. She stepped over the pool of blood that spread out from beneath Randy's head and tucked herself into the utility room. Kinsey sighed. *Such a mess in here.*

The exterior door to the backyard was unlocked, and she pulled aside the dusty curtain to peek through the dingy glass at the top. A clump of neighbors stood at the edge of the property.

Ah, Lucia Jones. Always were chasing after Randy. I wish you'd caught him.

And Chester Holiday. Biggest gossip in the neighborhood. Wonder what rumors he'll be spreading tonight? If only he knew.

The key turning in the lock caught Kinsey's attention.

A male voice. Must be one of the officers. "Mr. Gonzales. Please wait on the porch."

Footsteps.

Swear words.

They must have seen Randy.

The chirp and squawk of radios.

"Dispatch, we've got a 10-55d. Gonna need Homicide and Crime Scene out here... Copy that."

More footsteps.

The word 'clear' repeated several times.

"Oh, God. Hansen? I found the kids."

More radio chatter.

Footsteps getting closer.

"Where's the mom?"

"Do you think she…?"

"Haven't checked in here."

The door to the utility room flew open and two officers gaped at Kinsey.

It had taken a long time for the photographers to finish and the people in Tyvek suits and surgical booties to start their prowl around the house. Little yellow tents with numbers on them littered the rooms.

Finally, someone taped some paper bags over Randy's hands and tucked him into a body bag. The gun on the floor next to him went into another bag. The stretcher snapped into place and technicians wheeled him out.

Kinsey felt nothing and wondered if that was normal. She should have been upset. Instead, the Randy-shaped hole in her life was all fog and wind.

Another gurney appeared from the hallway, with a third close behind it. Tears streamed down the face of a man pushing one of the child-sized cadaver pouches.

A voice sighed heavily, right in front of Kinsey, so she shifted her attention.

"I'll never understand as long as I live how someone could do something like this."

Kinsey picked a sticky clot of blood out of her hair.

"Who found the bodies?"

"Her mother called for a welfare check. She was supposed to pick Ms. Lang up this afternoon but couldn't get in touch."

"What do you think set him off?"

"Who knows?"

"You get her feet."

Kinsey watched as they pulled her body out of the narrow utility room. She didn't recognize her own face. Her right arm caught on the edge of the washing machine, bending at a 90° angle between the wrist and elbow where the bone had been shattered. She winced.

Hours later, the crime scene investigators left. The officers left. Yellow tape fluttered in the October breeze.

"Mommy?" Joanna plopped down on the couch.

"What is it, baby?"

"Is Daddy coming back?"

Kinsey's eyes lingered on the glossy black pool of clotted blood where Randy had lain. "I don't think so, honey."

She thought a shadow swirled over it but told herself it was just the tree outside moving in the wind.

"Grandpa!" Charlie shouted.

Kinsey turned her head. "Dad?"

Her father stood near the front door, arms open wide enough to a hug all three of them. "Come on, Kinsey. Let's go home. Let's all go home."

October is Domestic Violence Awareness Month. If you are someone you know is in danger at home, please call the National Domestic Violence Hotline at 1−800−799−7233 or TTY 1−800−787−3224.

A Murder of Crows

By Artemis Greenleaf

Jim Bob Renfro needed a helper, and I really needed a summer job. His opening at *A Pest Free Palace* was available, and it paid $12/hour—a fortune to a high school sophomore with no experience.

Most of the time, I vacuumed up mouse turds and fetched things from the truck. Stuff like that. From the start, I didn't like Jim Bob—Mr. Renfro—much. Not sure why. He hadn't said anything mean to me, and he looked like an average middle-aged dude—nothing weird or creepy. One thing, though—he had a flashy gold watch that he was uber-proud of.

Once, he saw me looking at it and said, "You work hard, save your money, and maybe you can get a watch like this. It's very expensive."

What I was thinking was, "Did he really pay money for that gaudy bauble?"

I hadn't been there long when we went to a house for a follow-up visit. We climbed the rickety pull-down ladder to the attic to check the de-ratting progress. I had a trash bag tucked into my belt, and I held the flashlight for him while he rummaged around in a dark corner.

"Open the bag," he grunted.

He tossed a glue trap with an emaciated, dead rodent into the sack.

I felt queasy.

There was some rustling and squeaking, and Mr. Renfro produced a second glue trap with a terrified, live rat stuck to it, squealing and struggling to get free.

"You're not going to just toss it in the bag, are you?"

He cocked his head and looked at me as if I'd asked the question in Russian.

I pointed to the trap. "The rat? It's alive."

"And?"

"You're going to throw it in the trash and let it suffer?"

Renfro smirked and dropped the trapped rat onto the floor. Before I realized what he was going to do, he slammed his heel down on the rat's head.

"Now it's not suffering. Clean it up."

I gagged as I tossed the bloody mess into the garbage bag. *Maybe I should start looking for another job tomorrow.*

Renfro headed toward the ladder. "Put out some more glue traps."

I did. I just didn't remove the plastic layer that covered the glue.

By the time I came down and refolded the ladder, Renfro was finishing up with the homeowner.

"Good bye, Mrs. Thompson. We'll see you next week."

"Thank you, Jim Bob! I don't know what I do without you."

As it turned out, job opportunities were hard to come by, so I had to grit my teeth and stick it out for the rest of the summer. I was never so glad to see August roll around—couldn't wait for the first day of school.

It was a few months later when my mom called me to the phone. I think we're the only people I know who actually still had a landline.

"Hey, it's Jim Bob Renfro. Got a big job Saturday, and I wondered if you could use some extra cash?"

I could definitely use extra cash. "I have plans that night, but I'm free during the day."

It was Halloween, and Randy—one of my buds—was having his annual party. He and his brothers made their own haunted house in the garage with black plastic sheeting to form the corridors. Sure, sometimes it was cheesy, but they also had a pool, and it was still usually 80 or 90 degrees in October. And his mom went nuts with all the Halloween food. Spider cupcakes, mummy meatballs, witch fingers breadsticks. And then some.

"If we start by eight, we should be done in the early afternoon."

I was saving up for a car, for when I got my driver's license over the summer. I needed every penny I could get, because Dad said I had to pay the insurance, too.

"Sure. See you Saturday morning, Mr. Renfro."

"Crows. Filthy birds, even worse than pigeons. Started roosting on an office building, and we have to encourage them to leave."

"Oh?" I was afraid to ask.

"We have to install bird spikes, stuff like that. I'll tell you all about it Saturday."

Saturday was a little chilly, and I was glad I had a jacket when my mom dropped me off at *A Pest Free Palace's* office. Being here reminded me how much I hated this job. *Probably too late to call in sick.* I just had to think of the beautiful car I would buy with my saved-up money.

Mr. Renfro waved at my mom as he opened the door. She drove away. I wanted to run after her. But if I wanted my own car, I had to come up with the cash. I forced a smile.

"Morning, Mr. Renfro."

"Morning. Everything's already loaded up. Let's get 'er done."

The crow-plagued office building was across our small town, at the edge of the city park. Fifteen minutes after setting off, we arrived. A few of the black birds watched us from the trees as we tacked down bird spikes, installed rotating reflectors, and hooked up a motion-activated predator call broadcaster. Sometimes they flapped around and cawed to each other, but mostly they just watched. I felt like I was trespassing.

As I walked across the roof to string some cable, I heard a loud crunch and the roof started to give way. I threw myself backward and landed on my butt. At least my foot didn't go all the way through the shingles—just left a big dent. Renfro didn't ask if I was okay, but he did take a picture to send to the building manager to they could get a roofer up to repair it. Priorities, I guess.

When we finally got the equipment installed, we sat under the awning over the office's front door and took a break. I seriously wished I'd brought more than a PBJ sandwich and an apple.

"Now," Renfro said between bites of his own meal. "There's one more thing we have to do."

I'm not sure why this made the food in my stomach curdle. Maybe it was the way he looked at the watching crows.

"Pigeons, sparrows, they'd see all that stuff and just go away. Not crows, though. They're too smart for their own good. They'll find ways around the spikes, and realize the reflectors aren't a threat. Nope, crows, you have to send them a message."

I didn't like the way that sounded. I just nodded. Something bad was getting ready to happen. I could feel it coming.

Renfro packed up his lunch kit and took it to the truck. When he came back, he had a BB gun and a sparkly glass bead the size of a grape.

He chuckled softly. "They can't resist something shiny. Watch this."

Renfro rolled the bead out onto the grass beneath the tree where the crows were perched. They cocked their heads from one side to the other, trying to get a better look. After muttering amongst themselves, they hopped, branch by branch, to the lowest part of the tree. One must have been the lookout, because it stayed perched in the leaves and kept its beady little eyes on us while the other three flew down to investigate.

Renfro carefully sighted in on the middle crow in a group of three and *pop!* Down went the bird, struggling and flapping on the ground. The other three flew off, cawing loudly.

I don't think you should have done that.

He took the bird by the feet and carried up onto the roof. He used a heavy-duty staple gun to secure it to the roof, out of sight from the street, but easy to see if you were a crow flying over the building. It squawked both times he stapled it, and I jumped each time. I couldn't really see it, but I could guess what he was doing.

You really, really should not have done that.

"Welp, that's it. The crows won't roost here anymore."

He gave me $100 in cash and dropped me at my house—it was on my way back to his shop. The bills were new and crisp, but they felt dirty.

I tried playing *Assassin's Craft* online for a while, but I couldn't stop thinking about the poor crow stapled to the roof. My mom had dabbled in reupholstering chairs, so I found her tack removal tool and stuck it in my pocket, pulling my shirt over the long bit of the mini-crowbar that stuck out of my jeans.

"I'm going to ride my bike," I told my dad.

He barely looked up. "Don't be gone too long if you want a ride to Randy's at seven thirty."

"I know."

It took about twenty minutes to get to the office where we'd worked earlier, and dusk was just settling in. I didn't have a ladder, but I pulled the fire escape down and used that to get up on the roof.

There were crows everywhere. They surrounded the bird that Renfro had stapled down, and they moved silently out of my way as I approached their fallen comrade.

I pulled up the staples, and the bird just laid there limply. I thought it was dead, but one of its eyes opened. I didn't know what I was going to do with it, but I couldn't leave it there. I put it inside my shirt and tucked the shirt into my pants.

As I started toward the fire escape, a flash of something shiny and gold caught my eye. When I turned towards it, I noticed a huge hole in the roof, where I'd nearly fallen through earlier. *What had made it collapse?*

Curiosity was not my friend. I looked over the edge.

Lying on the polished concrete below was Mr. Renfro. *What on earth could have brought him back to the office building? He knew the hole was there—he took a picture of it.* I thought of the shiny object at the edge of the collapsed roof and swallowed hard.

I called 911and scurried down the fire escape.

The fire department broke through the glass doors, but it was too late for Mr. Renfro. They suddenly became very suspicious of what I was doing there. I called my mom to come get me, and I told them what had happened. Everything. I even pulled the half-dead crow out of my shirt to show them.

One of the police officers looked at him and said, "My girlfriend's a wildlife rehabber. Why don't you let me take him to her?"

I handed the bird over. *What was I going to do with it?*

Needless to say, I didn't make it to Randy's party. After taking such a long time to go to sleep, I was annoyed at being woken up at a quarter of six by cawing crows. Then came the pecking. There were birds pecking on my bedroom window. Irritated, I went to shoo them away.

I opened the window. "Let me sleep, you idiot birds!"

Something shiny glittered on the window sill. I rubbed my eyes and picked it up.

It was Mr. Renfro's watch.

CAMPFIRE

By Artemis Greenleaf

HALLOWEEN HAYRIDE
TOUR THE HAUNTED
WOODS
GHOST STORIES,
HOTDOGS, AND S'MORES
AT THE CAMPFIRE

WEN tapped the poster with his long fingers. "When are we going to get to the campsite? I'm starved."

"You're always hungry," I grumbled, then felt bad as I looked at his protruding ribs.

He shot me a sullen look. "Don't spoil my fun. I've been looking forward to this since the sign went up."

"I know."

We continued through the darkening forest. The few birds that hadn't headed south for the winter chattered as they bedded down for the night. A fresh breeze rattled the last stubborn leaves in the branches and knocked bare limbs together.

Wen licked his lips. "What kind of ghost stories do you think they'll tell?"

"Oh, I'm sure it'll be all the standard ones."

"What, like monsters in the woods?" he chuckled.

"Sure. People love monster stories."

The birds fell silent as we approached. The eerie scream of a fox echoed in the distance.

The trees grew denser and darkness settled around their feet. Leaves crunched and the occasional twig snapped as we walked along. The air was crisp and dry, smelling of leaves and dirt, with the occasional whiff of cedar or pine, carried on a gusty wind that wouldn't lay.

It got darker and darker, and we didn't seem any closer to the campfire. "We should have stayed on the trail, Wen."

"I'm taking a shortcut."

"We're not lost, are we?"

"Of course not!" He surged ahead of me.

We were definitely lost. "I wonder if they've started the fire yet. Maybe we can follow the smell of the smoke."

I sniffed the air, hopeful. But we were probably upwind of it still.

Wen snickered. "Worried about monsters? I think I smell a sasquatch."

"Ha!" He knows Big Foots—Big Feet?—give me the creeps.

I thought we sounded like a herd of elephants moving through the silent trees. If there were monsters hunting us, we wouldn't be too hard to find. Good thing there weren't any. Probably.

"Look over there." Wen paused and pointed off to the right. "I see a light."

"Looks a little small for a campfire."

"Of course, it's not a campfire. I think it's probably a flashlight. Or a lantern. Let's go!"

I crossed my arms. "Instead of chasing after some lone person in the woods, I think we'd be better off re-tracing our steps. Whoever that is might not even be going to the campfire."

Wen laughed. "Why else would anybody be out here in the forest tonight? It might even be the haunted woods tour. We could catch up."

I frowned. *Unlikely.* "Fine."

We followed the light for a while, but no matter how fast we moved, we couldn't seem to get any closer to it.

I stopped. "I don't like this, Wen. No way this is the tour group."

"But it could be part of the tour."

"I doubt that."

As if it heard us, the light turned in our direction. Instead of moving away, it was now drifting towards us, bouncing gently as if it were a lantern being carried along.

Were they lost, too?

Closer and closer. The light floated along about three feet off the ground, and I could make out a figure on the other side. It wore mist like a shroud, and its large dark eyes sank into its pale face.

Wen cocked his head and smiled dismissively. "Ghost. They can't do anything."

I wasn't so sure.

Without warning, the thing's face split in half and a tongue shot out, straight at me, like a giant frog's. It missed, barely, and I lurched backward, almost falling on my butt. The tongue was slithering on the ground, searching for something to grab onto, as I scooted backward. Wen banged an antler against a tree, trying to draw its attention. A second tongue lashed out in his direction, snaring one of his hands. Pulsating and twisting, it tried wrapping itself around his arm. He bit clean through the writhing flesh, and foul-smelling dark green blood spurted out. The creature cried out in pain, sucking both tongues back into its mouth.

It looked angry, and I didn't want to stick around for its next party trick. "Not a ghost! Run!"

We pelted through the trees like there was a wildfire behind us.

I'm not sure how long we ran, but the light didn't follow us. When I was sure it was far out of sight, I slowed to a stop.

Wen spat several times and wiped a glob of green blood off his lips. "Pah! That was horrible."

"Yeah? Well, you brought a souvenir." I pointed to his arm.

He snatched the piece of the creature's tongue that was still attached to this skin and pulled. "Ow!"

It finally came loose, leaving behind a bloody wound where it had attached itself, leech style. He tried to throw it away, but it stuck to his hand. I got a stick and prodded the viscid lump onto the ground. It wriggled wildly, and I covered it with leaves to keep it from sticking to anything else.

"Well, that was fun. Glad nobody else was around to see that debacle."

He shook his head and little bits of bark and a few leaves rained down. "How was I supposed to know that was going to happen? Do you think they'd have a tour out here if they knew there really *were* monsters in the woods?"

I shrugged. "Any idea what that was?"

"No. I've seen the lights before, but I've never gone close." He toyed absently with some of the hair on his cheek. "I have no idea where we are."

His stomach growled in an alarming way.

"Can you climb one of those trees, Wen? If we can find the road, we should have some idea which way to go."

He scampered up a tall pine freakishly fast. Bark nuggets fell in his wake, and the wind turned them into chunky shrapnel. Then silence.

I was just about to call out to him, when he said, "I see them! I can see the lights of the truck moving down one of the old logging roads. I see the fire, too."

Wen leapt off the tree from a much higher spot than I would have, and he landed with only the slightest rustle of leaves. Perhaps it was because he was so thin. I probably had at least one hundred pounds on him.

"This way!"

He jogged off, in almost the opposite direction we'd been heading. I followed. He hadn't set a fast pace, and I could run for miles, anyway. In this cool weather, it was a nice little jog.

Over the breeze and crunching of dead leaves, I heard a noise and raised my hand. We stopped. "Shhh! I hear people talking."

I veered left, toward the sound. Wen followed. He paused to raise his face to the gloomy tree canopy and sniffed the air like a dog. "You're right. I can smell the fire now. And food."

"You and food."

"Looks like they're just getting back from the haunted hay-ride—people are getting out of the trailer. Dinner time!"

We watched for a few minutes as pre-skewered hotdogs and marshmallows were handed out. There was a good crowd of people, maybe fifty.

Wen picked a cobweb-shrouded leaf out of my fur and dipped his antlers toward the campsite. "C'mon, Dogman. Let's eat!"

I smiled at my Wendigo friend, although my bared fangs usually made it look more like a snarl. "After you."

The Wendigo is a creature from the northeastern forests. The Algonquian people recognized him as the spirit of desolate places, the personification of the famine of winter. His insatiable hunger for human flesh makes him a fearsome enemy who can eat people, or possess their bodies and use them to commit atrocities. He is often depicted as having a human body with antlers on its head, or a deer's head and antlers. There is a psychiatric condition known as Wendigo Psychosis—the overwhelming desire to eat other humans. In 1878, a Cree man named Swift Runner suffered from this when he murdered and ate his entire family over the winter.

Dogman sightings are most frequently reported in the Midwest, especially Wisconsin and Michigan, although they have been described on every continent except Antarctica. In 400 B.C., the Greek physician Ctesias wrote about tribes of Cynocephali, or dog-headed men. Christopher Columbus and Marco Polo both reported encounters with them, and Saint Christopher, patron of travelers, has the head of a dog in some early depictions. Most dogmen seem to prefer living in rural areas and forests, but they have been sighted in large cities. The dogman is described as having a hairy, bipedal body with the head of a dog or wolf. It may or may not be a werewolf, but it is definitely not a Big Foot. Linda Godfrey has collected accounts of numerous dogman sightings in her book, *The Beast of Bray Road*.

The Will-O-The-Wisp, or ghost lights, has been encountered by people outside at night for at least as long as folklore has existed. Explanations range from trickster faeries leading travelers astray, to restless ghosts, to swamp gas (and many things in between). Since they have a habit of disappearing when people try to get close, no one has ever really seen what is behind the light. The Marfa Lights and the Bragg Road Ghost Lights are two Texas examples of this phenomenon.

Possum Pete's Premium Pizza

By Artemis Greenleaf

A GOL plastic coin sailed through the air and hit Emily just above the ear. "Hey! Watch it!"

The herd of six-year-olds cackled and ran back to the ball pit.

Emily sat at the table, folding arcade tickets with her sister. "I can't believe you're having Kaden's party here. You should take full advantage of it being the day before Halloween. Go full on spooky. There's already so much going on, you don't even have to plan the parties."

"You can't beat Possum Pete's Premium Pizza Party Package," Beth replied with a snicker. "Kaden loves trick-or-treat so much. Seems like a shame to try and cram the holiday and his birthday together."

Emily raised an eyebrow with mock indignance. "What? You don't want parenting tips from your childless sister?"

"Ha. At least his birthday isn't in December."

"Yeah. Happy Birthmas, Sis."

One of the staff came and whispered in Beth's ear.

"Come on, Emily. Help me round up these hooligans."

Kaden was reluctant to leave the ball pit, until his mother said it was time for Possum Pete and cake. Then he leaped out and ran back to the party room. Beth and Emily seated the kids at a long table with butcher paper on it before going back to the sparsely populated adult table.

The staticky speakers blared a fanfare. With a click, a spotlight shone on the stained red carpet near the 'Employees Only' door. A man with a top hat, red and yellow striped trousers, and a red jacket came out of the door and strode up to the stage, the spotlight lighting his way.

Is he a ringmaster or an MC?

The man raised a microphone. "Ladies and gentlemen! Let me present to you the one, the only—Possum Pete!"

Kids screamed and clapped their hands.

The spotlight whipped back to the door, and a six-foot opossum, unobtrusively led by a staff member, shuffled up the carpet and stepped onto the stage. Emily took an immediate dislike to the shopworn costume. Its grin seemed more of a leer to her, and it had way too many teeth. It was indistinguishable from a giant rat—the only clue was in the name.

But the kids chortled at his failed stage magic and guffawed at his corny jokes. After his five-minute stand-up routine that only a six-year-old could love, the sparkly black curtain opened to reveal a band of animatronic monsters.

A hobgoblin was up front with a shiny red guitar. Behind him, a tall, oddly proportioned man in a black suit, red tie, and no face stood at the keyboard. Opposite him, Bigfoot sat in front of a drum kit, sticks in hand. A grey alien with an over-sized head and huge, glossy black eyes played bass guitar, and a girl in a dirty white nightgown, dark hair brushed in front of her face, stood center stage with a mic in her hands.

Bigfoot tapped out a cadence on his sticks and the group started their set. Children's songs, traditional and sanitized pop. The kids swarmed the small dance floor in front of the stage to run around to the music. While what they were doing could only be described as dancing in the loosest of terms, they were having a blast.

I would have been terrified of this group when I was Kaden's age. Emily studied the machines. They were really well done. Not a faux fur seam to be found, and their motions were smooth enough to create the illusion that they really were playing the instruments.

Guess animatronics have come a long way since I was a kid. She recalled the dusty, jerky creations from her own childhood. They were intended to be a cartoonish bit of fun, but Emily had found them to be nightmare fuel. Still gave her the heebie-jeebies.

After six songs, the players froze and the curtain closed. Sweaty children piled back into their chairs, ready to be recharged with cake and punch.

Emily checked her text messages. Her Tinder date just canceled on her. Apparently, his mother was in the hospital. She wondered if that was true. Sighing, she set the phone on the table before she got up to put the candles on the cake so the kids could sing *Happy Birthday* to Kaden, with special guest performer Possum Pete.

Fifteen minutes later, the refreshments had been demolished and parents began to arrive to collect their cranky, cake-smeared children. Two hours at Possum Pete's Premium Pizza takes a lot out of a kid. They'd been overrun with fun.

The last of the guests left and Beth retrieved a collapsible wagon from her car to transport the mountain of gifts and miscellany. Emily helped her load it up, then unloaded it into the back of the SUV while Beth strapped Kaden into his booster seat.

"You coming to the house, Em?" Beth pushed the button to close the liftgate.

"I don't know. Kaden looks really tired. Bet he just wants a nap."

"That makes two of us."

"Three of us, actually. But I've got to go home and get more resumes out. If I don't find a job soon…"

"You know you can always stay with us."

"It may come to that." *But I really, really hope not.*

Beth hugged her sister. "Thanks for coming to help out. See you later, Sis."

Emily got into her car and reached into her bag for her phone to select a playlist. It wasn't there. *Must have left it on the table.*

She rushed back into the restaurant, grateful she hadn't removed the neon wristband that proved, at a glance, that she'd been vetted and approved to enter.

The young woman at the counter grinned. "How many coins can I start you with?"

"I was just here, and I think I left my phone on the table. I'll run back to the party room and get it."

"Wait a minute! I'll get someone to look."

But Emily hurried past the cashier.

When she opened the door, she wished she had waited.

Bigfoot sat at one of the tables, his legs stretched out on several chairs, and a large soda rested next to his hand. The girl in white was gesturing wildly in a silent conversation with the alien. The hobgoblin and the eerie man were playing cards.

Emily blinked and shook her head, then jumped as the party room door slammed. She spun around to see the MC standing behind her.

"Why did you come back here?"

"I-I left my phone." Emily's voice was small and shaky.

He scanned the tables and spotted the device. Then he raised his arm, and it flew into his hand. "This phone, Emily?"

Emily nodded, tears welling in her eyes. "How-how did you know my name?"

He raised his eyebrows. "Mysterious psychic powers. That and it's on your nametag."

She raised her hand and patted the *My Name Is* sticker on her chest.

He shook his head. "Maybe it's just as well you walked in. Come on. I'll introduce you."

"What?"

"I'm St. Germain, by the way. We have to talk about what's going to happen next, and you need all of the information you can get."

Emily blinked again. *Can too much sugar make you hallucinate?*

He led her to the card players. They were the closest.

"Hey, guys. I'd like you to meet Emily." He put his hand on the shoulder of the faceless man. "Emily, this is Slenderman, but you can call him Slen."

Slen reached out with his over-long arm and took her hand into his large, icy fingers for a moment. Emily heard his tinny voice in her head. *Nice to meet you.*

"And this handsome fellow is Puck."

The hobgoblin rose and gave her a little bow.

"Nice to meet you. Puck? You mean like…"

He pursed his lips. "Yes, that Puck. William Shakespeare has a lot to answer for."

Emily scrubbed her hands down her face. "I don't understand what's happening. You seem very nice, but you-you can't be real. Sorry. I'm not trying to be rude."

It's okay. Slen's voice echoed in her skull. *We are real, even if you've been told otherwise. I was not born, not like Puck here. I am an egregore.*

"A what?" Emily said out loud.

St. Germain patted Slen's shoulder. "An egregore is a living thing that is created by the concentration and focus of a large group of people. You know, like Santa Claus."

"Santa? He's—"

"Yes. He is now. Didn't use to be. Anyway, after that internet art contest where Slen was created, so many people started focusing on him that they thought him into existence. Thoughts are things, after all. The reason he's in hiding is that some really twisted people have been trying to invoke his power to do really, really terrible things. He's not like that. He can't help the way he looks."

It's true. That viral picture of me standing on the playground? I wasn't there to hurt those children. I was there to protect them. Nobody saw that creep sitting in his car watching the kids. But I knew he was there.

Emily shook her head quickly. "This is a lot to take in. I... Did you say 'in hiding?' Here, at a pizza place?"

St. Germain chuckled. "Sometimes the very best hiding places are the ones in plain sight. As far as most people know, we just have excellent animatronics."

Was that fruit punch spiked or something?

She jumped when St. Germain replied out loud, "No, Emily. The punch was not spiked. You just came back here when you shouldn't have."

Puck cleared his throat. "I'm here because someone's trying to capture me to use my body parts in some crazy black magic ritual. Only have another five years before they kick the bucket. Death told me so himself."

"That sounds dreadful. Being hunted like that."

The hobgoblin nodded. "It is."

St. Germain took Emily's arm. "You need to meet the big guy."

Bigfoot swung his feet off the chairs as they approached and took a sip of his drink before he rose to his nine-foot height and extended a massive hand.

"Cuthbert, at your service."

"You're… British?"

"It's not so much that our race is British, but that we learnt English from British people. But of course, that was back when English was mostly a grab-bag of Saxon, German, French, and Scandinavian. The Vikings weren't just Norwegian, you know."

"It's… it's very nice to meet you, Cuthbert."

"As it is you, Emily. Although I wish it were under better circumstances."

"Oh?"

"Yes, I'm afraid there is a million-dollar bounty upon my head. Normally, humans are easy enough to avoid, but this one particular hunter has set up sensors and traps directly in front of my portal. Preposterous! Not sure if he's a wily old thing or just dead lucky."

Emily looked at St. Germain. "Portal?"

"Yes, they are trans-dimensional beings. But there are certain access points, keyed to their energy signature, that allow them to come and go on this plane."

Her eyes widened as she turned to Cuthbert. "And you can be killed when you're in our world?"

"It depends. In some cases, yes. But it would be far worse to be locked in a cage and experimented on for the next hundred years, don't you agree?"

"I can see your point." Emily took a surreptitious sniff of the air. "I hope you don't think I'm being rude. That isn't my intention at all, so please forgive me if it seems that way. But many people report a horrendous smell when they have Sasquatch encounters. And you smell, well, like a very expensive cologne."

Cuthbert bellowed with laughter. "Don't worry. I have heard this question many times before. The odor comes from an electro-chemical reaction from the portal activating, not us. Well, not most of us. There is this one chap from our tribe… Now, you probably know this already, but if you haven't time to shower, spritz your hairbrush with a bit of cologne or perfume before you brush your hair, you will smell delicious all day long."

Emily giggled. "I'll keep that in mind. Thanks for the tip."

"My pleasure."

St. Germain took Emily's elbow again. "I need to finish the introductions."

Cuthbert gave them a slight bow and a flourish of his immense hand.

"Now," St. Germain whispered in Emily's ear. "Kameko is very sensitive about her appearance, so tread carefully."

"Got it."

St. Germain gave a little bow. "*Konnichiwa*, Kameko. I would like to introduce you to Emily."

Kameko returned the gesture. "*Arigatou*, St. Germain. Is Emily to be joining us?"

"Perhaps. We shall see."

"It's my pleasure to meet you, Kameko."

"Why is that?" the girl asked sharply.

Emily swallowed. "It's not often one gets to stand in the presence of such an ethereal creature as yourself."

Kameko tilted her head to one side, and then the other. "Thank you, Emily. I wish those who are trying to trap me inside a glass jar to throw into the sea felt as you do."

Emily bowed to Kameko.

A harsh, buzzing voice entered her head. *Hello, Emily. You may call me Jake.*

Jake the alien?

Humans cannot pronounce my actual name, so I have chosen this one.

Sorry! I'm not used to people reading my thoughts.

Most humans aren't.

St. Germain glanced at his watch. "Jake is here to avoid vivisection by the US military."

Emily winced. *Nice to meet you, Jake*, she thought as St. Germain led her away.

He sat her down at a table in the corner. "Now that you have met our guests, it's time for you to decide."

"Decide what?"

He fiddled with a button on his coat. "Obviously, we can't just let you walk out of here."

"Why not? Who would believe me if I told them?"

"There are spies everywhere, and not every person you see is human."

Emily leaned back in her chair. "What does this mean? You're going to... kill me?"

"That's up to you. You can agree to the enchantment and work here in the restaurant, helping out with both our human and non-human guests. It pays well and you get to meet a lot of interesting... people."

"What enchantment?"

"Even the most well-intentioned person can slip up. You will only be aware of our supernatural guests when you are at work. When you are not in the restaurant, they will be blocked from your consciousness. Also prevents spying. Every single human employee in this building has the enchantment."

"Why can't I get the enchantment and *not* work here?"

"Because the spell needs to be charged regularly. It takes a lot of energy."

Emily rubbed her chin. "And if it runs out of charge?"

"You die."

"And if I don't agree to the enchantment?"

"We go through an unbelievable amount of pepperoni here."

Emily shuddered. "Doesn't sound like much of a choice."

St. Germain shrugged. "It is what it is."

She thought about her big orange cat, Rufus, lounging in her apartment. If anything happened to her, Beth couldn't take him in—her husband was violently allergic to cats. Emily couldn't stand the thought of her sweet kitty going to a shelter. Besides, wasn't she planning on spending the rest of the afternoon job hunting anyway?

"Okay. When do I start?"

Cheating Death

By Claire Murray

Geez, kid. What'd you have to go and shoot him for?" Willie pushed Bobby away from the clerk's body and out the door of the convenience store.

"'Cause he was gonna shoot me! He pointed that rifle right at me." Bobby's voice shook as much as his hands.

Willie took Bobby's gun and stuffed it in his jacket pocket, almost crushing the three packs of cigarettes and map he'd just stolen. The other pocket held a stolen pint of whiskey. He looked around the empty parking lot and surrounding street. "Waving that gun around, you'd have every cop in town on us in minutes. I already got all the cops in Ohio chasing me. Find us a car. We gotta get outta this state fast."

Minutes later, Willie jimmied open the door of a '94 Honda Accord parked outside an auto body shop. He leaned over and unlocked the other side and hotwired the engine before Bobby was in the car. For a big man with a hefty beer belly, he moved faster than the younger, skinny, tow-headed Bobby. Heading northwest on Route 27, Willie lit two cigarettes and handed one to Bobby to help calm his nerves. Bobby coughed on the first few puffs but kept smoking.

Willie drove just under the speed limit, stopped at all the stop signs, and slowed down as he passed a group of older youth in gaudy Halloween costumes, capes and sheets fluttering in the late-evening breeze … anything to avoid looking like he was in a hurry to get away. He figured the teens were returning from the youth center party he'd seen advertised in the convenience store. *Typical small town event. Keep the kids out of mischief so they won't grow up to be criminals, like me.*

Both stiffened when two police cruisers screamed past them going toward the store they'd just robbed—and Bobby had shot the clerk. Willie looked at Bobby. Sweat and a trickle of tears streamed down they boy's face. *Why'd I ever hook up with this baby-faced piece of trouble?*

Willie hoped his nephew's stupidity hadn't hammered the final nail in his coffin. He flicked his cigarette out the window and turned to Bobby, his voice weighted with years of smoke and whiskey. "What you gonna do now? Piss your pants? It's over. You did it. Learn to live with it."

"That's easy for you to say, Uncle Willie. You been in trouble all your life. Me, I never done nuthin' like this. Never. It's like Momma always said. 'Uncle Willie is trouble. Stay away from Uncle Willie.'"

Willie kept his eyes on the road and ignored the growing whine in Bobby's voice as he talked through his tears. "Why'd you give me a loaded gun? You said it wasn't loaded … it was just to scare people. Well, here's a news flash. It scared someone. ME. Now I've killed somebody and I'M GONNA DIE." He broke down in sobs.

Willie said nothing to console him, just kept driving as tree-lined streets with homes and businesses became large stretches of farmland. Highway 27 offered few turnoffs and little traffic this late in the evening. Willie stepped on the gas, eager to get away from Ohio and all the trouble he'd been in there throughout his life.

Start over, that's what I need to do. Get outta this state. By now, cops'll be hitting the highway. He turned left onto an isolated westbound street. Crossing the north/south railroad tracks, he figured he was close to the Indiana border.

Bobby stopped crying long enough to ask, "Where are we, anyway? I never been this far away from home. Where we going?"

"Goin' nowhere and everywhere, kid. I'm wanted in Ohio, so we'll cross the line up ahead into Indiana. But shooting that clerk this close to the border? Well, you made it a little bit tougher for me to get away from my past. So we'll—Damn! We're almost out of gas. Kid you have brought me nuthin' but trouble since I picked you up at your Momma's funeral last week. I don't know why I bothered."

He steered the stolen car into a cornfield before it stopped on its own. "This'll hide it a while. Stuff that loot in the backpack and strap it on. We walk from here."

Cornfields on both sides offered a place to hide if anyone came down the road, which ran straight as far as they could see. They followed it, eventually turning south with the road. A few hundred yards farther, another road intersected. Willie looked around, calculating their next move. Southeast led to a nearby farm. Northwest, farther away but in the direction he wanted, silos from another farm silhouetted against the night sky. He didn't care about Bobby's sore feet and headed northwest. They could hide in a barn and rest while he checked the map to see how close they were to the border. There wasn't enough moonlight to see it well on the road, and the stiff breeze would blow out his matches.

Willie cautioned Bobby to remain silent. "Sound travels far when there's nothing to block it. And see that small house ahead on the right? It's close to the road. We don't want anyone hearing us. Stay on the paved surface and keep quiet."

They passed the house in silence, advancing to the farm ahead on the left, and took shelter between several metal silos and the large electrical unit that seemed to manage them. It was enough cover for him to light a match and check his map.

"The border's close, Bobby—walkable. But it's all farmland. The closest town is some place called College Corner, a bit north. From there, we can hit the county road. It goes straight west and meets the north/south highway near Liberty, Indiana. The farther away we can get from the border, the better."

Bobby nodded, his mouth stuffed with food. He swallowed and said. "I'm sorry I caused so much trouble ... shooting that man. I was scared, Uncle Willie."

"Yeah, kid. I know. First time's the worst. Gotta shake it off, though. Let's rest. Then maybe I can find a car that'll get us there quicker."

Willie awoke, alarmed at first that he'd fallen asleep in the middle of a getaway. The whiskey bottle was almost empty. *Strange, I don't remember drinking. I always remember drinking. And I don't drink in the middle of a getaway.* He shook off the prickly feeling along his neck and stretched to warm himself. Bobby dozed nearby.

Willie used the silos for cover to scout the farm. Set back from the road, the large farmhouse was dark. Several vehicles were parked alongside. When the clouds parted, he saw another building to the left and headed for it. A singsong voice spoke *in* his head, stopping him mid-step. His ears heard nothing but crickets and bullfrogs.

"Willie ... Willie Collins. I've come for you."

"Who? ... What? ..." Willie completed his step and looked around. Flattening his back against a silo, hand on the gun he'd taken from Bobby, he inched around the silo, expecting to find a farmer with a shotgun. *But this farmer knew my name. How ...?*

"Willie. Turn around."

Willie whirled and faced a cloaked figure, face unseeable except for grinning teeth. Taller than Willie. Taller than anyone he'd ever seen. The figure shook its fist at Willie, who shivered as fear and nausea washed over him. Teeth chattering, he summoned his courage and asked. "Who ... who are you? What do you want?"

"Why, Willie, I want you." The faceless mouth smiled, showing yet more teeth. It raised an arm and the bony, clawed hand reached out for Willie. He stepped back and fell on his back, stomach jiggling upon impact. He could not take his eyes off the apparition, which chuckled at his misstep. "I've been looking for you. You're on my list. Taking that man's life moved you up ... to tonight."

"Wait! I didn't ... I didn't kill him. Bobby did. My nephew Bobby. He shot the man."

The apparition chuckled again. "Do tell. You gave him the gun, told him it wasn't loaded. You are responsible for the clerk's murder. And here you are, selling out your sister's son, the boy you swore you would protect if anything ever happened to her. You are quite a man, Willie. You'll do just fine in my entourage."

The apparition reached out again. Willie pressed himself back into the dirt, unable to let out the scream that sought release. As suddenly as it appeared, the apparition vanished.

Bobby ran to Willie's side and gaped at the sight of his uncle shaking in the dirt and swearing. Bobby helped him stand and they returned to their temporary shelter.

"What happened, Uncle Willie? You were talking real loud. You could'a got us caught."

"You ... you didn't see it? You didn't see that Thing?"

"What thing? You were talking to the air. I woke up and went to find you. What happened?"

"Never mind. We gotta get out of here. This place is ... well, never mind. I ... I gotta change. Give me a minute."

Willie walked away with the backpack and changed his pants and undershorts, swearing the whole time. "Bloody hell, blaming me for Bobby's stupid mistake." He swapped out the items in his discarded pants, looking at the time on his burner phone. *Twelve-ten. Twelve-ten AM. It's morning. That Thing said "tonight," but it isn't tonight any longer. It's a new day. I just Cheated Death.*

When Willie returned to pick up their things, Bobby asked him why he seemed so cheerful. Willie smiled. "It's just my lucky day, dear nephew … new lease on life, that sort of thing. Let's clean up and not leave any clues that we were here."

He picked the lock of the storage building he'd seen earlier, took two full gas cans, and put them in the back of the truck with no alarm that was parked beside the house. Breaking the collar lock and setting the truck in neutral, he and Bobby pushed it down to the road. Willie hotwired it and they took off for the Indiana border. "Man, this is too easy, almost. Like my new lease on life has turned my luck."

He searched the radio for a suitable station while driving fast over the country road. "What'sa matter kid? You keep lookin' at me funny-like."

"I never seen you like this, Uncle Willie. Well, ain't seen much of you the past ten years. But all week you've been this grumbly kind of person and now … you're … happy? I don't get it."

"I was in the joint most of that time. It gets to ya. Not much to be happy about when you're in the joint or on the run. Since I been out, well, I'm on the run again, ya know?"

Bobby still stared at him. "Yeah, but somethin' happened to-night. Somethin' you're not telling me. You were talking to yourself back there. And you looked Real Scared."

"Me? Scared? Yeah, maybe. At first. But then … then I looked at the time, boy, the time. Everyone's got a date with Death. You never know when it's comin' but it is. But what happens when Death comes and the time slips by? What if your day is today and Death is late? Can you Cheat Death? Do you die or do you live? I just found out the answer, Bobby. And the answer is—What the—"

Willie swerved to avoid hitting the apparition in front of the truck. It swerved with him, and he drove off the road into a tree, narrowly missing the sign that signaled their passage into Indiana.

The apparition chuckled. "No one cheats Death, Willie. You and Bobby were on my list for Halloween Day. When you crossed the border, you crossed time zones, and it's only eleven-thirty PM central standard time in Indiana …. still Halloween Day. Welcome to my entourage."

Cheating Death:

Copyright 2014

This work was originally published in Kings River Life Magazine (2014)

Reprint with permission from author, October 2022

About the Author

Claire A Murray is a native New Englander living in Arizona where she writes crime, mystery, and fantasy novels and short stories. She is a member of Sisters in Crime, Mystery Writers of America, and the Short Mystery Fiction Society. https://cam-writes.com

Wish Me Luck

By A.B. Richards

THE man with the greasy hair grinned. "I guess today's your lucky day."

I tested the zip ties around my wrists. "Really? You said you were going to kill me."

He chuckled. "Never said it was *good* luck."

Slipping a rough hand between my arm and bruised ribs, he hauled me to my feet.

The burning pain in my side forced a gasp out of my mouth. I had been trying to be stoic. Thought maybe if he didn't know how much pain I was in, he wouldn't be tempted to poke the bruises. I might have been wrong about that, though.

"Don't worry. We're going to have some fun first. But not here. Too close to the trail." He picked up the shoe that had come off my foot when he dragged me into the bushes and tossed it near me. "Put it back on. No clues left behind."

"How am I supposed to do that with no hands?"

He glowered for a moment. "If you try anything funny, I'll break your leg."

I believed him. He was at least double my weight and maybe as much as a foot taller. I scanned the environs for any offshoots or paths while he tied the laces.

The man stood up and grinned at me. "No one's ever going to find you." He chuckled again. "Or me. The Law's too stuck on technology." He gestured to the trees. "All you have to do is go off the grid and you may as well not even exist. I can do anything I want, and they can't do jack about it."

"I'm guessing you know something about those other three hikers that have gone missing over the last two months, then."

He snorted. "That's only the ones you know about."

This well-maintained trail was popular among hikers, runners, and cyclists, but the surrounding forest thickened to a gloomy wood on either side. Dense shrubs and fallen trees made it almost unnavigable, but the man picked his way through the underbrush as if he knew where he was going.

He probably lives out here in some Unabomber shack.

"I got a promotion at work. More money, and closer to my house. Really lucky to get it."

The man grunted. "Why you tellin' *me* that?"

"Because I was supposed to meet my mom for dinner tonight. I was going to tell her about it, but… well, I felt like I needed to tell someone."

He grunted again.

"I don't suppose you know anything about rare coins, do you?"

"What?" He pushed a branch out of the way for us to pass.

"Yeah. It was the weirdest thing. I was really low on cash a couple of weeks ago, so I scraped together all my loose change and went to the grocery store to put it in the coin sorter thing—you know what I'm talking about? The machine that takes your change and gives you a voucher or gift card you can spend at the store?"

"Yeah."

"Anyway, there were a couple of coins that got rejected. One of 'em, I'm not sure where it came from. Don't remember seeing it before. Kinda goldish or coppery circle in the middle, and a silver circle on the outside. Writing on it isn't English. Thought I'd find somebody to look at it and tell me if it was worth anything."

He snorted. "Probably a Mexican peso. Looks like your luck has taken a nosedive."

"Maybe. But—"

"Would you shut up? I don't care about your life."

"Don't you? You're trying to steal it."

He stopped and spun me around to face him. "Enough!"

He raised his fist, but only glared at me. I stumbled as he shoved me forward into the thicket. My head throbbed. Not sure how long I'd been out after he hit me over the head from behind, but it was a while. Hadn't expected that, but probably should have.

It wasn't easy to tell how much of the gloom was shade from the trees and how much was from the vanishing sun.

A thorny vine stretched its rigid stems like a razor wire spider's web from a nearby tree. I managed to scratch up my leg as we pushed on through the thicket, and blood trickled down my calf. *Enough for a marker?* I brushed away the clot as often as I could to keep it flowing.

I wiped my jaw across my shoulder to dislodge some dried mud. "So, you live around here?"

He growled like a grumpy dog.

A stick snapped somewhere to my left. Something large was moving through the underbrush.

The man heard it, too, and frowned at the dusky woods. He muttered to himself, and I thought I caught the words, "feral hogs," but I couldn't be sure.

"One of them survived, you know. She dug her way out of that shallow grave you left her in and crawled to the highway. That's how I knew you were out here. I'm lucky you finally took the bait."

He squinted at me, working his jaw back and forth, testing words in his head and biting them back. "Lucky?" he spat. "I'll make sure *your* luck runs out. Double-damn sure. Then I'm on the wind, and nobody will ever find me. I'll hunt again wherever I please."

He took a moment to smirk before he shoved me again, and we resumed shuffling through the fallen leaves.

And there it was, maybe fifty yards ahead. As predicted, the Unabomber shack.

"Looks like a fixer-upper."

"Shut it," he snapped.

A deer stepped onto the rough path between us and the shack. It was over-sized for a native whitetail and shadows wrapped around it, even in the clearing, scoffing at the dwindling light.

The man waved his arms. "Get out of here! Go on! Git!"

The deer lowered its head and shook its antlers.

"Frickin' ruttin' bucks." He cast around for a weapon. Not much but vines and forest litter presented itself.

The deer took a few steps toward us. It was just wrong. The creature was bone-thin and its limbs didn't fit its body. Didn't look strong enough to hold up its heavy rack of antlers. The poor thing's face was so skeletal it appeared not to have any flesh on it at all and its eyes were sunken deep into its head.

The man shook his head. "Don't worry, dude. I'll put you out of your misery soon enough."

"Bet he just needs food. He looks really hungry."

"Naw. He's had all summer to fatten up. That there's chronic wasting disease. Zombie deer sickness."

Wonder if anyone's thought of that for Halloween—Zombie deer.

He waved his arms again and ran a few steps toward the deer. "Get out of the way!"

It continued toward us.

The man looked around again. He broke off a small limb from a yaupon bush. Couldn't have been any thicker than my pinkie finger, but it was long and bushy.

"Nice flyswatter."

He shoved me and I toppled over. I wriggled around until I could see what was happening.

The man charged, waving the branch. The deer rose onto its hind legs, towering at eight or nine feet tall over the man.

He froze.

And it kept walking.

The man took a few steps back.

Instead of dainty cloven front hooves, the deer had gnarled, clawed hands. Thick, iron-like talons sprang from its knotty fingers.

And still it came.

The man made a gurgling scream and tried to flee, but he tripped over his own hubris and sprawled in the fallen leaves.

I shook my head. *And he thought he was such a predator.*

Fading sunlight glistened off strings of slime as the monstrous deer opened its jaws. Its eyes glowed a deep red.

Unable to get up, I watched in morbid fascination as the thing's nightmarish spikey teeth were fully exposed.

It bent over the fallen man. He screamed and struggled, then went limp. When the beast raised its head again a few minutes later, the lower third of its face was smeared in gore.

It rose and approached me.

The creature stank of rot and decomposition as it leaned over, running a rough hand down my arm. Its wicked talon sliced through the zip tie like hot butter.

"Thank you. I wasn't sure that vine had drawn enough blood to open the portal for you to come."

I put my hand over the strange coin in my pocket, to make sure it was still there before I stood up. I had started seeing the monster standing under a tree across the street that night after I returned from the store with my paltry coin-bought groceries.

It had called to me in my dreams.

It knew what I wanted, and it told me what it wanted, so we struck a bargain. One blood sacrifice for one wish. I figured I could kill two birds with one stone—give some monsters to the monster *and* get something for me in exchange.

As long as I had the coin, it couldn't hurt me, so why not?

It continued to loom over me.

I got to my feet and dusted pine needles off my butt. "That was a little harder than I expected. I'd been coming out here so much without him showing up that I'd started to think he'd moved on. Hadn't counted on him bashing me over the head, though. Good to be lucky, I guess. But you got your meal. Now, it's time for my wish."

"This will be the second. You have one left, Detective."

Lechuza

By Artemis Greenleaf

I T was hot, for October. Just a little over a week before Halloween, and it was still 90 humid degrees on the Texas Gulf coast.

I sat on the patio, fan on and iced tea in hand. My mom's two foo-foo dogs, Alice and Charlie, panted near the sliding glass door. No one knew their exact parentage, but they were small, white, and fluffy. Mom adored them, but I preferred dog-sized dogs to these snack-sized fur nuggets.

My aunt, who lives in Oregon, had heart surgery, and Mom volunteered to stay with her for a couple of weeks while she recovered. I was voluntold to petsit Alice and Charlie while she was away. I didn't mind, actually. My SO, Chris, and I were going through a rough patch and, frankly, we could use the time apart.

So here I sat, on a Friday evening, drinking iced tea, listening to an audio book, and trying to cook dinner in the outdoor kitchen. I had ditched my work skirt and heels for shorts and flipflops the instant I walked through the door, and weekend mode had taken hold soon after. I could play the book as loud as I wanted, because the closest neighbor was half a mile away, and no one would eavesdrop on the spicy romance I was currently consuming.

The gas grill had a trick to it, and I hadn't mastered it. There had to be more temperature selections than "Off" and "Incinerate," but for the life of me, I couldn't find them. I was about to give up and go into town to see what I could find—this was *terra incognita* to GrubHub—when I heard it.

A baby crying.

Alice growled, her hackles rising. Charlie tucked his tail and whimpered.

"Shhhh." I shook my head at the dogs, then peered into the gloom. "Hello?"

I turned on the backyard lights. The open grassy area was lit up like a Friday night football field, but the trees cast eerie shadows that moved and flickered in the night breeze. Not even the halogen penetrated the thicket at the edge of the property, and I felt uneasy, as if I was being watched.

I listened again for the baby, but only heard a few crickets.

"It was just some animal," I assured the furballs. "A rodent, probably. C'mon pups. Let's go inside."

I made sure the gas grill was off, and the dogs scrambled inside the instant I pulled on the door. Giving one last glance over my shoulder before I followed them inside, I saw nothing unusual. I did, however leave the outside lights on.

I was looking for my car keys when my text chime went off. It was Chris. The part I could see read, "I really need to tell you something…" Was he going to tell me he missed me and couldn't wait for me to get back? That he was glad I was gone and hoped I could stay longer? Not entirely sure I wanted to see the full message, I tapped on the text bubble icon.

"I really need to tell you something. I'm sorry. Moving out. I've met someone. Sorry."

That explained a lot. Honestly, I felt more relieved than sad. I suppose I'd known for some time that we weren't right for each other. I just hadn't wanted to admit it. Inertia can be a terrible thing.

How should I reply? It wasn't that I didn't care, but nothing I said was going to change anything for either of us. "Fine. Whatever."

It would be weird, going back to an empty apartment. But I would be fine. Better than fine. I might even stop by the shelter on the way back and adopt a kitten. Chris hated cats. Ha. Maybe I'd get two.

That didn't solve my immediate problem, though.

"I'm going to get dinner. You two be good," I told the dogs as I turned on most of the downstairs lights.

The truck stop hadn't changed much since the last time I was there, years ago. Fried everything. Large portions. Quart-sized red plastic tea glasses. This week's special was the gizzard platter—greasy, gristly globs surrounded by mounds of fried pickles and French fries. With thin, brown gravy. My years away at college and living in Houston had bent my taste buds in a different direction, and I now had a difficult time finding something on the menu that appealed to me.

"Sue? Good gosh almighty! Your mother didn't tell me you were in town."

I looked up to see that my waitress was Margarite Tremont, one of Mom's oldest friends.

"Yeah. I'm looking after her dogs while she's taking care of Aunt Cynthia."

"That's right. I knew she was going out of town. Didn't think about the critters. Know what you want, darlin'?"

"Um, I think I'll have… the grilled cheese on wheat bread with a dinner salad." I knew the salad was a risk. Hopefully, the lone tomato wedge would be closer to red than green.

"Sure thing. Iced tea to drink, right?"

"Yes, ma'am."

"How could I forget? You and Cody were so close for so long."

"Right." I smiled and nodded.

It had almost seemed like fate—our moms were best friends, and we'd known each other since we were babies. We thought we'd stay together, long distance, as we headed out to different colleges, and we did at first. But we inevitably drifted apart.

"I'll go get your order turned in. Food'll be right out."

"Thanks, Miz Tremont."

She winked at me as she tucked her order book into her apron pocket and made her way back toward the kitchen, pausing to fill a tea glass here and take another order there.

I sat and continued reading that steamy romance on my phone while I waited. I was just getting to the good part when I heard the loud clearing of a throat. Irritated, I looked up.

"'Scuse me, Miss. Is this seat taken?"

"Cody?" Wow. He'd filled out a lot since the last time I'd seen him. He wasn't the lean, lanky young man I remembered. Still lean, just not lanky. *Did his mother text him and tell him to come here?* "Of course! Sit down. I didn't know you were…"

"With the po-lice?"

"The uniform looks good on you." *Really good.*

His mother came by with another iced tea. He raised it, as if in a toast. "How've you been?"

"Good. How about you? Mom said you got married."

I hadn't meant to blurt that out. I was in grad school when she told me, and I was too busy to think much about it then. Or maybe I just didn't want to.

"I did. But Kelly and I had… irreconcilable differences. Didn't quite make our first-year anniversary."

"Oh. I'm sorry."

We spent almost two hours catching up. I could have talked longer, but I was starting to yawn, and the puppers still had to go out to do their doggy business.

He walked me to my car. "Drive safe, now."

I almost told him about the baby crying earlier, but decided it was silly. "I will."

I didn't see or hear anything unusual when I took the doglettes out. In fact, there was nothing unusual for the next three days. Other than Cody and I texting each other every evening.

On Tuesday night, I was almost asleep when I heard a thud, then it sounded like a herd of buffalo was running across the roof. Charlie and Alice hid under the bed. Apparently, discretion is the better part of valor when you're a mini-pup.

"Come on, you two. It must be the wind blowing a tree limb across the roof. Don't be so silly."

I got up and pulled back the curtain. Nothing moved under the moonlight, although dark clouds smothered the starlight to the west. I closed the drapes and slipped under the covers, pulling them up to my chin. The roof stomping died down after a few minutes, but my light stayed on all night.

I invited Cody to the house for dinner Wednesday night. When I went to turn Charlie and Alice out in the back yard, he said, "They shouldn't go out without supervision. There's coyotes around. And owls. You'd be surprised what they can carry off. And you should be careful, too. One of your neighbors went missing Friday night. Personally, I think he just skipped town to get away from the repo man. But you can't be too careful. I've been driving by, before my shift ends. Just to make sure everything's okay."

I wished he would stay over, but he had to work. At least there were no roof walkers that night.

Cody was going to pick me up on Friday to go out. I was almost ready when I heard a knock at the door. I glanced at my watch. He was fifteen minutes early. I started down the stairs to let him in when Alice ran in front of me and bit my ankle, hard enough to draw blood.

"What is wrong with you?" I shouted at her.

She only growled in response.

I went the other way, into the bathroom to get a bandage. By the time I came back, she was nowhere to be seen, but I did hear nails clicking on the hardwood floor below. *Maybe I should call the vet in the morning to make sure she's current on her rabies shots.*

"Coming!" I shouted, hoping Cody could hear me as I hurried down the stairs.

Earrings in my hand, I opened the front door. Cody wasn't there. No one was, and there was no car parked in front of the house. I slammed the door and locked it, then turned on all the downstairs lights, and the outside lights, for good measure.

When Cody arrived ten minutes later, Charlie and Alice greeted him like he was their long-lost best friend.

He looked around at all the lights. "Everything okay?"

"I thought you were at the door a few minutes ago. I heard a knock, but there was no one there."

He stepped outside and looked around for a moment. When he came back in, he held a nut. "You got that big ole oak tree that overhangs the front porch. It is fall—there's acorns everywhere on the ground. I'm sure that's all it was."

"You're probably right." It was then I noticed the dark circles under his eyes. "Are you okay?"

"Yeah. Long night. There was a traffic fatality just down the highway. Driver swerved off the road. Maybe trying to avoid a deer or something. She was more messed up than she should have been—I guess the smell of blood attracted scavengers before anybody found her."

I shuddered. *How awful.*

All the lights stayed on. I didn't want to come back to a dark house.

It helped that Cody came in with me after our evening at the dance hall. Poor guy. He was so tired he'd fallen asleep on the couch by the time I got back into the living room with two glasses of wine. I covered him with an afghan and went upstairs. I will say that I slept better with him in the house, and I would wake up to face the monsters refreshed.

Saturday was Halloween, and Cody was working a double shift. I was surprised at how many kids fit in the back of a pick-up truck to come around to the houses out in the sticks for trick-or-treat. The candy ran out around nine and I turned off the outside lights. I had skipped dinner, and for a while, I didn't miss it. By 10:30, my stomach was growling and I was low on groceries. The only solution was to drive to the truck stop for another grilled cheese. Nothing else was open, and that can of mushroom soup in the Mom's pantry just wasn't going to cut it.

When I returned to the house, I parked in the garage and come through the back door. I was glad of the garage, because the wind had picked up clouds had billowed in. The dogs were silent. That was unusual. I caught a glimpse of something moving in the living room. My heart skipped a beat.

Was that lightning, or someone shining a flashlight in through the window? Fight or flight kicked in, and I chose fight. I'm not sure why. I charged to the window and was horrified to see the pane sliding up, and long fingers creeping under the sash.

Mom didn't have security cameras, but I did have my cell phone. I wanted to have a photo to show the cops, so I took several shots with the flash on. Then I called 911 and put the phone on speaker.

The long fingers were slipping away, and I wanted to try and catch this punk. Maybe I could even hold him until the cops rolled up.

"No!" I yelled, grabbing a couple of the fingers and pulling them backward against the wall as hard as I could. Anger flowed through me, and I was more than happy to hurt this jerk trying to break in to my mother's house. Thunder grumbled in the distance.

The dispatcher stayed on the line with me, and I shouted answers to her questions through gritted teeth. I dropped the phone so I could push down on the window to keep the burglar's arm trapped. As red and blue lights strobed down the lane towards the house, he gave a final desperate wrench and pulled his arm away, disappearing into the dark.

I opened the front door as Cody and another officer ran up onto the porch. I told them what happened. The other officer went to see if he could track the thief while I showed Cody the photos.

"I know it's Halloween, but if this is a joke, it isn't funny." he said.

"What?" I looked at the screen and almost dropped the phone. Staring back at me was a pale, wrinkled face, eyes clouded as with cataracts, but a black, vertical pupil was clearly visible. Instead of a nose or mouth, it had a curved, sharp beak. *A Halloween mask? Was this some sick prank?.*

Something dark lay on the window sill.

"What's this?" Cody picked it up.

It was a large feather, black horizontal bars on a grey background. *What was it from? A hawk? An owl? If it was from an owl, it was a huge one.*

Outside, a baby cried, then the sound was lost in a boom of thunder. The windows rattled.

"Brooks!" Cody called out. The other officer hadn't returned from his search, and it had been twenty minutes.

I didn't want to be alone in the house, so I walked around the property with him, looking for Officer Brooks. There were only four city police officers. Two were here, one was on the way, and the other was on vacation. Cody had called the county sheriff for reinforcements, but they were a half hour away.

We looked all night in the rain for Tony Brooks, and a search team combed the area for two weeks, but he was never found.

But that all happened a long time ago. Cody and I got married not long after that and had four beautiful babies. Now, our kids have grown up and flown the nest. Cody died in a car crash... has it been two years, now? They never did figure out what made him swerve off the road. But I'm not alone. On short autumn nights, the owls sit outside my window and call to me. Someday soon, I'll join them.

Seventh Circle

By Artemis Greenleaf

Mr. Hughes loved Halloween.

He once told me that it had been his wife's favorite holiday, and he kept up the decorating to honor her after she'd died. An elaborate shrine to the dead, if you will. Instead of "Sweets for the sweet," "Deads for the dead?"

But I digress.

Every year, he created a different theme. Last year had been the best yet. A realistic cemetery erupted from his yard one morning. Bats hung from the trees, and giant spider webs stretched between tombstones. On Halloween night, he added a fog machine, and a hidden projector threw stalking specters against a nearly invisible mesh. Younger children were too scared to come close to the trick-or-treat bowl, but the older ones loved it—it was almost like a free haunted house.

He always made a costume that matched the decorations. One year, I helped him pass out candy, and he was surprisingly good at making me up like a zombie. I caught sight of myself in the mirror and it terrified me for a moment before I realized that it was me. The makeup was too realistic, too perfect. Made me think of the nightmares I used to have when I was in the hospital. I didn't sleep that night. Or the next one. By the time I got to fifty-six hours, I was starting to hallucinate. I collapsed on the sofa and slept twelve hours straight. But at least I was too tired to dream. Another plus: my house was incredibly clean and my closets were more organized than they'd ever been.

The year after that, he did a werewolf scene. A disguised post supported a leaping canine monster, and I couldn't tell you how creepy it was to go to my mailbox and be faced with a werewolf in mid-attack. Did I mention that it moved? It gave me the hee-bie-jeebies. Reminded me too much of the time my aunt's big dog attacked me when I was little. Still have the scars on my jaw. I even go the long way around out of the neighborhood, so I don't have to drive past that monstrosity on the way to work. I couldn't even look out the living room window in the evening—those glowing eyes haunted my nightmares.

Aside from his Halloween obsession, Mr. Hughes isn't a bad neighbor. If you don't mind obsessive grass mowing. At seven in the morning. But he always smiles and waves when he sees me. Although I suspect he might have been the one to complain to the HOA about my edging. That's how the lawn service company does it. Not my fault, is it?

But this year, he's got the most over-the-top tableau I've ever seen. And that's saying something, given his decorations. It looks like a scene from Dante's Inferno. Layers of ragged nylon fabric dance in the breeze of a fan, simulating flames. Damned souls writhe in the fires, and motion sensor-triggered sound effects wail in anguish. An enormous three-faced Lucifer head with pointed teeth and gaping maws was tethered between the two oak trees.

The night he put out the display, I woke up screaming. It had been months since that happened. I had to call my shrink at three AM. I think it's probably been two years since the last time I had to do that.

Mr. Hughes. It was almost like he knew. Knew my most vulnerable spot, then gleefully sucker punched me. Was he trying to drive me insane? He couldn't possibly know. But why? Why on earth would he choose this scene?

Surely, if he had been there, listening to my wife and kids screaming as the house blazed around them, he wouldn't have done it. There was nothing I could have done as I lay on the ground, grass slick with my own blood, jagged bone ends sticking out of my thighs. I had tried to drag myself to the front door, but my legs were worse than useless. An explosion—later I found it was a gas line—shattered the windows and roared through the house like the Devil himself. I had been upstairs and got thrown through a picture window into the front yard. I lived. Not sure if it was a blessing or a curse. I had survived Hell, and for what? To be mocked by Halloween decorations? But this year, I could do something about it. I called up Mr. Hughes and offered to help with the final touches.

Sunday, Halloween morning, was cool and dull. Thin clouds lazed by, briefly exposing the wan sun. Clots of neighbors paused on the sidewalk, admiring Mr. Hughes' pièce de résistance. A very realistic corpse had been added to one of the jaws of the three-faced Satan. The body's head and neck vanished into dark mouth, and the arms were raised, hands against the teeth that were trying to chomp it down. The grass had been torn up, as if there had been an epic struggle. The character wore the kind of robe common to Christmas pageants—perhaps he was meant to be Judas? But I'm not really sure. Almost as soon as I'd arrived at Mr. Hughes' house the prior evening, he'd offered me whiskey from an expensive, imported bottle. We each had a shot, then another. We went outside to look at the display, and he told me that this would probably be the last year of his Halloween extravaganzas. I agreed, fingering the length of clothesline I had in my pocket.

Watching from my darkened window, I could see that the neighbors' concern increased to panic as Halloween evening stretched on, and Mr. Hughes had not appeared to pass out candy. I saw Mrs. Montoya, his other next-door neighbor, standing on the sidewalk in front of his house, talking on her cell phone. I went to see what she was up to.

She ended the call before I got out there, and as I got closer, I could see that she was crying.

"What's wrong, Mrs. Montoya?" I kept it formal—I didn't know her all that well.

She sniffled before she turned to me. "Ernie seems to be missing—he hasn't come out with candy, and he won't pick up the phone. I've called the police. I'm afraid he may need to go to the hospital."

Too late for that. "Really? Why?"

"He was diagnosed with an aggressive pancreatic cancer. He only had a few months to live."

"I didn't know. I'm very sorry to hear that." *You have no idea how sorry.*

I sat on the curb and started to laugh. I was still laughing when the police arrived.

Takeout

By A.B. Richards

Nikolas Pendragon adjusted his cravat to hide the bloodstain. He'd have to remember to stop at the 24-hour drugstore on the way home to get more hydrogen peroxide.

He stifled a yawn and set the empty wineglass on the table, a tiny red clot clinging to the rim.

Why did I even come here tonight? I've taken on too many website design clients and I'm so tired. He rubbed his eyes. The Halloween Ball was *the* event of the year, and he would be conspicuous by his absence.

A young woman in a purple corset and black lace dress sat down next to him. Her arm was bandaged at the crook of the elbow, and she looked a bit too pale.

"Are you alright, Drusilla? You didn't over-donate again, did you?"

She gave him a demure smile. "Not this time. My brother just got out of the hospital, and I've been helping take care of him. Haven't been getting enough sleep."

"Oh? I hope he's okay."

"He had back surgery—a herniated disc. First few days were kinda rough, but he's getting around better now."

Her fingers lazily traced a path along the end of her collarbone toward her throat, across to the other clavicle, and back again.

He swallowed but didn't take his eyes off her hand. "I, uh, hope he heals quickly." The gentle throb of her carotid artery with each heartbeat mesmerized him.

"Thank you, sir."

He closed his eyes so she couldn't see them roll up to the ceiling. "You don't have to call me that."

"Lord Lazarov might say otherwise."

Nikolas' lips pressed into a straight line. *Lord Lazarov' was born Timothy McCain in Baton Rouge, Louisiana, and only started dressing like a goth after his aunt left him a pile of money and a lovingly restored Victorian mansion in Houston.*

Drusilla bowed her head slightly.

He shrugged. "As you wish."

The door to the back parlor opened and Lord Lazarov himself stepped out, his silk waistcoat completely unbuttoned, his white linen shirt only half buttoned and his top hat askew. Two young women, one in a French maid outfit and the other in a form-fitting black dress with a neckline that plunged dangerously close to her navel, followed him out.

Lazarov scanned his subjects as if taking inventory, then sat in an ornate chair at the back of the room, not far from Nikolas and Drusilla. The Lord licked his lips and bared his very expensive custom vampire fang veneers. He clapped his hands twice.

The dim ambiance of the room dimmed even further, and a spotlight shone in the center of the floor. Two well-chiseled men and two equally athletic women stepped into the brightness. They wore zentai suits—covered head to toe in black matte spandex— and looked like a group of shadows that had escaped their owners.

They stalked each other around in a circle as the music started, then the men did backflips toward the center, each one ending up in a full backbend with the crowns of their heads together. The first woman cautiously approached, then chose a man, put her hands on his chest and lifted herself into a handstand. She walked toward his abdomen, then lowered her legs backward, placing her feet on his hipbones and peering out between her knees.

Nikolas looked away. Contortionists gave him the creeps.

He leaned over to whisper to his companion. "Ashley? You're a very sweet girl."

"Drusilla."

"Drusilla isn't real. Ashley is. And I worry that things are going to get out of hand and Ashley is going to get hurt. You know Lazarov, and all these people, are really only interested in one thing, right?" He swept his arm around the room. "Everything else is just set decoration."

She caressed his thigh. "What makes you think Drusilla isn't interested in that one thing?"

He put his hand over hers and held it in place. "Drusilla might be. But Ashley is the one who will pay the price if—"

The table shuddered as an acrobat landed on it right in front of Nikolas and Drusilla. The contortionist dropped to her stomach, curled her legs up until her feet rested on her shoulders, then blew a kiss at Nikolas before she twisted away and rejoined her fellow performers.

"Then make me yours," Drusilla purred in his ear.

He ran the backs of his fingers along her jaw, down her throat, and finished at the little hollow where her collarbones didn't quite meet. "You don't want that."

"Don't I?"

The quiver of her heartbeat under his fingers was sublime. Nikolas closed his eyes and rose. "I have to go."

He felt Ashley's eyes on his back as he wove his way through the other party guests on the way to the front door. He could feel her pain at his rejection in that gaze as well, and he was almost angry with her for touching him that way, putting him in such a mood.

Dressed in a Victorian-lite outfit with a neckline that bordered on obscene, Sangria Morgellon blocked his way at the door.

"What's wrong, Nicky? Couldn't work your wiles on the new girl?"

"I'm going home."

"Alone?" Sangria opened her mouth to reveal her own faux fangs.

Nikolas studied the over-done makeup on her face and the not-quite-top-quality wig whose best days were behind it and thought of all the reasons he disliked her.

"Come on, then."

She took his arm, and they walked through the double-wide front door.

Nikolas ran cold water into the stoppered sink. He unwound the cravat from his neck and dipped it in the water before scrubbing the bloodstains with soap. He left the tie to soak in its chilly bath while he hung up his waistcoat, double-breasted tailcoat, and pin-stripe trousers. He'd bought the pants in London and was particularly fond of them. Made by Queen Victoria's personal tailor, so they were of exceptional quality.

Now in his boxers and undershirt, he pulled on his bathrobe and tied it loosely at the waist. Nikolas smiled as he pushed his tired feet into his absurdly fluffy slippers. He sauntered into the living room and relaxed into his recliner, pushing the button until his feet were comfortably raised off the floor. Nikolas wiggled his toes in the fur and smiled—best shoes he ever bought.

He looked at his watch and scowled. Less than an hour before the oppressively cheerful sun rose above the horizon.

Sangria's body lay face up on the other side of the room, two perfect holes at the base of her throat. He didn't have time to properly dispose of her now. This is why he much preferred eating out to bringing food in. He'd sleep now, but he'd better get it handled tonight. The cleaning lady was due tomorrow.

He wiggled his toes in his furry slippers again, smiling as he turned off the lamp in his windowless room to sleep.

The Veil

By Artemis Greenleaf

Y OU know what they say about Halloween, right?" Missy asked.

"What's that?" Jacob replied.

"That the barrier—I think it's called the veil—between the world of the living and the world of the dead thins enough for ghosts to get through. You think that's true?"

Jacob signed quietly, more of a gesture than a sound. "I wouldn't count on it. I know how much you miss your sister, but… well, I just hate to see you get your hopes up for nothing, that's all."

Missy fidgeted, and a frown flickered across her face. "There has to be a way. You hear about people seeing ghosts all the time."

Jacob reached out and stroked her cheek with the backs of his fingers and gave her a half smile. "Come on," he said, reaching for her hand. "We spend too much time here, and it only makes you sad."

"I wanted to be here when they installed the grave marker, wanted to make sure it was right."

Jacob nodded. Missy took his hand and got up from the metal bench that overlooked the family cemetery plot, running the fingers of her other hand over the top of the granite tombstone as she passed it.

"You're probably right. We should go."

The house was dark when they got back. Dark on the inside, anyway. Security lights lit up carefully selected bushes in the front yard. One of them highlighted a wooden pumpkin on a stake with a cutesy, grinning black kitten on top. "Happy Halloween!" it exclaimed to the neighborhood.

"I think we ought to see a professional about contacting my sister," Missy said, pulling a curtain back to peer out.

"Fine," her husband replied. He knew that when Missy made up her mind about something, there was no talking her out of it.

By early afternoon, Missy had an appointment with Madam Celestina. The medium seated herself at a round wooden table in a cheery room with antique pictures on the wall. A smoky quartz crystal ball the size of a large grapefruit glistened in a shiny black stand in the middle of the table.

Jacob had refused to come.

"I need to talk with someone on the other side," she told Madam Celestina.

The psychic advisor leaned forward, and the large jewel in her red satin turban glared at Missy like the eye of an ancient idol. "It can be done. But there are no guarantees," she replied. "It makes a difference if the person you wish to contact also wishes to contact you."

"I'm certain my sister would want to hear from me."

The psychic raised an eyebrow. "Perhaps. It is easiest, then, to make contact in the dark before the dawn. Sometimes, it may help to go to a favorite place of your loved one. Don't be too disappointed if she doesn't respond. She may not be able to hear you."

"Could you try something like a séance?"

The psychic shook her head. "Séances and Ouija boards are more effective for contacting localized entities—those just hanging around or passing through the area—rather than specific individuals. I have also found that when people are in a hypnogogic state, they are most receptive to messages from the other side."

"I'm sorry. Hypno what?"

"Hypnogogic. That's when you aren't really awake, but you're not really asleep, either."

Missy nodded. "I never knew that had a name." She looked down at that table and traced the wood grain pattern with her finger. "My sister, Linda, was due to have a baby when the accident happened. I was already feeling bad because I had scheduled the shower so late, and Jacob and I had just picked up the invitations from the printer on our way out to dinner. Then everything's kind of a blur. I think the police said the driver was drunk, but I can't quite remember. So many things happened that day—I just get confused about everything."

The psychic touched Missy's hand. "I know. Sometimes death seems so unfair, and we have a hard time understanding it. But it is possible to make contact across the veil. It may take some practice, however. When you wish to make contact, you must focus on the person you seek—much like tuning in to a radio station. If it makes you feel their presence more, you can go to one of their favorite places."

"Thanks," Missy said as she stood up to leave. "I appreciate the help."

"Feel free to contact me any time," the psychic said. "Have a blessed day."

"Perhaps we're just early." Missy frowned and looked around the park. "I can't understand why no one is here. There is always a barbecue on the Saturday after Franco's birthday. Always. I would think that this year, it would be even more important than ever to have family and friends around to remember the dead."

Jacob squeezed her shoulder. "Not everyone grieves the same way, Missy. It might be more painful than helpful to do it so soon after the funeral."

Missy turned to Jacob. "Maybe. Besides, no one specifically said anything about having the barbecue at any time during the wake or after the funeral. It's always done. I just assumed…"

"You know what they say about assuming."

Missy whipped her head to the left. "Did you see that?"

"See what?" Jacob turned his head in the direction where Missy stared.

"There was a movement—a shadow—off to my left. There's nothing there now, though."

"I didn't see anything."

Missy scanned the area before turning back to her husband. Her head jerked away again, this time to the right. "There it is again!" She pointed over his shoulder. "Do you think it could be Linda? Maybe she knows I'm trying to contact her."

Jacob shook his head gently. "Maybe. I didn't see it, though. It could also be your imagination working overtime because you want to see your sister so badly."

Missy scowled at him. "Just because you don't think I can reach across the veil and contact Linda doesn't mean it isn't so."

Jacob's eyes tracked left, and he turned his head.

"You saw it, didn't you? That shadow moving just at the corner of your eye."

"There's nothing there."

Missy gave him a sly smile. "Sure. Of course not."

Jacob ran his hand through his hair. "Look, no one's coming. We should probably have tried to confirm this thing before we came all the way out here. I think we ought to go home."

Missy smiled as she slipped her hand into his, and they left.

"It's Halloween today. Maybe it'll work this time."

"Missy, I've been trying to humor you, because I know how much you miss Linda. But this has got to stop. This obsession just isn't healthy."

"I don't need you to tell me what to do," Missy snapped. "I'm going to contact my sister, whether you like it or not. You don't have to participate."

"I'm not trying to boss you around. I just think you're too close to this and you aren't being objective. You've put so much effort into crossing the veil that I'm concerned about your mental health." Jacob squeezed her hand. "Linda was like the sister I never had. I miss her, too. But I love you, and I don't want to lose you as well."

Missy regarded Jacob for some time. "Perhaps you're right. I want to try tonight, because I think it's my best chance of making contact. But maybe after that, we should go. Leave this place. There are too many memories here, too many reminders…"

Jacob put his arms around Missy, but she wasn't comforted.

Late afternoon shadows stretched across the grass as Missy and Jacob sat on the wrought-iron bench in the cemetery.

"Are you sure this is the right place? Seems to me like an odd place for her to come," Jacob said.

"She'll be here. I can feel it."

In the near distance, a car door slammed, then another. Footsteps crunched on gravel. Muted voices. A baby crying. Silence. Missy sat forward on the edge of the bench, expectant.

No one came.

The orange sun kissed the western horizon, and the shade of the cemetery trees deepened into shadow.

Soundlessly, a pale figure moved down the paved walkway toward Jacob and Missy.

"Jacob, look! It's Linda."

He nodded. "So it is."

Missy rose and moved toward the bare soil of the grave, her hands resting on top of the granite headstone.

The gate creaked as Linda pushed it open. She looked so pale in the dusky light that Missy felt a twinge of sorrow. Linda carried a bunch of white roses in her left hand.

"Linda!" Missy called.

Linda looked around, but didn't stop. She knelt down at the headstone, dropping the flowers at its base. Then she pulled a soggy tissue out of her pocket and dabbed at her eyes.

"I'm so sorry," she said. "I didn't mean to go into labor the morning of the funeral. I wouldn't have missed it if I hadn't been in the hospital. But you would love your niece. She is so beautiful. Well, maybe her hair is a little wild. But we've named her Melissa Jacqueline, after you and Jacob."

Good Help is Hard To Find

By Artemis Greenleaf

WATCH out! Watch out! Watch out!" Cassandra shrieked. The African Grey parrot ruffled her feathers and hopped onto a brightly colored ladder in her cage, her red tail flicking in the air.

Marianne looked up, not pausing her potato chopping, and shook her head.

"Ow!"

The knife smacked against her fingernail. It stung, but there was hardly a scratch. Now if it had been half an inch over… She grimaced. Just the thought of the knife slicing through her flesh made her shudder.

"What's gotten into you, you crazy bird?" Marianne resumed her chopping.

"Hey, hey, good lookin'!" the bird replied.

Marianne looked around the kitchen. "You're probably missing Daddy as much as I am. Must be strange for you to be without him. Jeremy and I'll do the best we can to take care of you. Never had a parrot before, though."

"I'm gonna kill you. Kill you!"

"What did you say?"

"Kale! Kale! Cuuuuuuucumber! Cumber! Cuke! Cuke! Cuke!" Cassandra climbed on the bars and scraped the metal with her beak.

"No kale, and you ate all the cucumber yesterday. I have some carrots."

The bird squawked, then she whistled. "Collins! Collins!"

Toenails clicked on the hardwood floor as the German shepherd mix trotted into the kitchen, his tail half-wagging.

"That was mean, Cassandra. Now I'm going to have to give him a treat, too. He gets his first."

She scraped the potatoes off the cutting board and into a pot of hot water, then put a lid on the pan.

Marianne retrieved a piece of chicken jerky for the dog and a carrot for the parrot. Collins trotted into the living room to enjoy his. Cassandra clutched the vegetable in one foot and waved it around, the ferny green foliage at the top bouncing like a pom-pom.

The curtain rings scraped against the rod as Marianne pulled them aside to let in some light. *I don't remember this house seeming so dark before.*

She'd spent holidays and summer vacations at her grandparents' home, but never lived here. When they both died unexpectedly in a car crash, her parents had moved in, but Marianne had already left for college by then. Now that they were gone, the place had fallen to her.

The gothic mansion had way more space than she and her husband needed, and she'd been toying with the idea of making it into a bed and breakfast. Marianne hadn't even gotten around to looking in all the rooms yet to see what, if anything, her parents had done with them over the years.

Jeremy swept into the kitchen with some bags of groceries. He kissed her on the cheek before he began unpacking them.

"Think I found everything." He handed her a plastic sack of broccoli crowns.

"Good. Guess that'll be our local store now."

He forced a smile. "Sure. If we can figure out how to pay the taxes on this place."

"We'll find a way." Marianne hoped she was right about that.

"Hmmm." Jeremy set a bottle of shiraz on the counter.

Huh? Marianne whirled around. A chunk of carrot had bounced off her arm and now rolled on the floor.

"You're gonna kick it. Kick it!"

Jeremy squinted at the bird. "What?"

"Twelve! Eleven! Seven! Three! Four! Twenty-Seven! That's the ticket! That's the ticket!" Cassandra flapped her wings.

Jeremy's brow furrowed. "What is that bird talking about?"

Marianne chopped the broccoli into florets. "Not sure… wait a minute. Daddy used to play the lottery with our birthdays. Mama was born December 11th, I was born July 3rd, and Daddy's birthday was April 27th. Wonder why he taught her those numbers?"

"Ticket! Ticket! Kick it!" Cassandra replied.

Marianne chuckled. "We may need a lotto win for trick-or-treat tomorrow. Have you seen the price of candy?"

Jeremy grinned. "I'll do it. Right after supper, I'll go get a ticket. I forgot the candy, anyway."

"Daddy played those numbers for years. Never worked for him."

"Probability says all number combinations will come up eventually."

Marianne lifted the lid and stirred the potatoes. "It's your two bucks. If you want to take financial advice from a parrot, that's up to you."

"Marianne? Marianne! Look at this!" Jeremy's hands shook as he held out the lotto ticket in one hand and his phone in the other.

She spat out her toothpaste before she took the ticket and compared it to the numbers on the screen. 27. 3. 11. 4. 12. 7.

"Is this a trick?"

He threw his arms around her waist and spun her around. "Seven million dollars, baby!"

"I can't believe this." Marianne shook her head, then pinched herself. "Ow!"

"I'm callin' in sick! We'll go down to the claims office as soon as it opens." He kissed her mouth, too hard, before bringing his cell up to dial his work number.

Marianne finished getting dressed and hurried downstairs for breakfast. She frowned at the peanut and sunflower seed shells and wood splinters on the floor around Cassandra's covered cage. But after her lotto picks, Marianne could forgive her anything.

"It's dark in here! Dark! Dark." Cassandra croaked.

"Okay, I'm coming." Marianne took the drape off the bird's large cage.

"Hey, hey, good lookin'!"

"Good morning, Cassandra."

The parrot flapped her wings and blinked in the sudden light.

Marianne gave her fresh water, opened a can of food for Collins, and measured some kibble into his bowl. She whistled and called his name.

He did not come.

She walked around the lower floor, empty dog food can still in her hand, calling for him.

She rounded a corner and almost dropped the can. A shadow loomed behind the lacy curtain.

Marianne's heart pounded. *Is someone trying to break in?*

Something hard scratched on the glass.

She took a step backward and tried to scream, but only a hoarse squeak escaped from her mouth.

Woof! Woof!

"Collins?"

She snatched the filmy curtain back from the window and saw the dog standing on his hind legs, paws against the window. He barked again.

"How did you get out there? Did Jeremy let you out to pee-pee and forget about you? Figures."

Marianne returned to the kitchen and let the dog in. He nuzzled her hand for a moment before trotting over to his food bowls.

The aroma of coffee pervaded the kitchen. *I don't remember starting the pot.*

She turned around to see an older woman, almost as grey as her uniform dress, wiping her hands on her crisp white apron.

"Angelique! You startled me. I'm not used to having…"

"Employees living in your house, ma'am?"

"Yes. Listen. Did either you or Barnabas let the dog out this morning?"

"No, ma'am. My husband's busy polishing the silver this morning."

"Please call him in here. We got in so late Wednesday, then you guys were off yesterday. I haven't seen him since last Christmas."

"Yes, ma'am." She glanced at the dirty dishes in the sink. "I'll go and fetch him. It's a very large house, and there's only the two of us, after all."

"Well, since we—" Marianne stopped herself. *Probably best not to blab about the lotto money.* They hadn't even claimed it yet. "I'll speak to my husband. It *might* be feasible to hire some more staff."

"Very good, ma'am."

Marianne stared after her as the housekeeper set off in search of the butler. Like Cassandra, they'd come with the house, and the estate included a fund to pay their salaries for the next ten years. They'd been with her father at least that long, the last ones left after he'd gradually let all the other staff go.

Most of the cash that Marianne had inherited had been used to clear up some deferred maintenance issues her father had left behind. Living in a castle sounded like a fabulous idea—until it needed a new roof and a fresh coat of paint to make it habitable.

A cat meowed, loudly.

Collins scattered kibble as he jerked his head up. Marianne turned to search for a clandestine feline but saw no sign of one.

Cassandra chuckled, then meowed. "Here, kitty, kitty."

"Silly bird. You're such a—"

Marianne froze.

A large black cat sat outside the French doors that led to the covered patio. Not a sleek, well-fed indoor cat, but one with a tattered ear and a lean, scarred body. A ray of sunlight shone through one of its glass-green eyes, causing it to glow. She swallowed hard. He looked like the kind of cat who'd shred the face of anyone who got too near.

And he sat. Staring in and disapproving of her.

Beyond the patio, the sprawling estate had largely returned to the wild. The pool had gone an alarming shade of green, except for the area where the cascading rock fountain churned the water. Tall grasses had taken over the lawn, their dry brown skeletons dancing in a puff of breeze. Wild grapes strangled unidentifiable trees. A fallen hackberry tree blocked access to a paved pathway. *Probably take a machete to get to the tennis court, if it's even still there.*

"I'm sorry, ma'am, but Barnabas has left to do the shopping."

Marianne whipped her head around. "Angelique. I wish you'd make a little more noise. You scared the cra—crackers out of me."

"Sorry, ma'am."

"It's alright. Doesn't matter. Did my father have a cat?"

"Not exactly. There are some ferals..."

Made sense. The estate had gone feral, so of course street cats would take up residence.

She turned back toward the doors, but the cat was gone.

"Stop it! Stop it! Stop it!" Cassandra shrieked.

A coffee mug shattered on the tile.

"So sorry, ma'am. The handle was slippery. I—"

"Marianne? You ready, babe?"

"Be right there, Jeremy," she called to him before turning back to Angelique. "We'll be out, probably at least the rest of the morning."

"Very good, ma'am."

It had taken far more than the rest of the morning. First, they went to see a friend of Jeremy's who was a tax attorney to set up a trust. Then off to the bank to set up an account for the trust. Then to the lotto claims office with all the forms and receipts to collect the prize.

It was early evening and the sun floated just above the horizon as they pulled onto their street. Roving bands of small children in costumes, trailed by groups of adults, dotted the sidewalks.

"Glad you got that candy last night." Marianne smiled at the clumps of revelers. She'd wondered if chauffeurs would drive the children from house to house in this neighborhood.

Marianne yawned as they waited for the iron gate to open. She'd make sure Angelique and Barnabas were prepared to pass out candy to the trick-or-treaters before she and Jeremy headed upstairs to the jacuzzi tub with their bottle of champagne.

The kitchen was both immaculate and quiet when they came in, almost tripping over Collins, who was curled up by the door. Cassandra sat on her main perch, eating a slice of cucumber.

The bird whistled. "What did you do? Do? Do?"

"Nosey." Jeremy tapped the cage as he passed.

Cassandra flicked her tail. "How do you do? You do?"

Marianne covered the birdcage. "Goodnight, Cassandra."

"Now what? Now what?"

"Now, you sleep."

Jeremy put his hand on one of the French door handles. "I'll just take Collins out for a few minutes. Meet you upstairs." He flashed her that million-dollar-smile. Or seven million, as the case may be.

She grinned back at him, trying to stifle a yawn, and left to locate their employees.

"Angelique? Barnabas?"

The living room was lit up, but twilight had already settled in most of the hallways. A scratching noise caught Marianne's attention. *Don't tell me we have rats, too.*

She followed the sound toward the library. A man stood at the end of the corridor.

"Barnabas?"

He didn't reply but exited toward the game room.

Marianne followed. *What has gotten into him? Is he angry with us for some reason?*

She flicked on the lights. The game room was empty. She also checked the sitting room, the portrait gallery, and even the conservatory while she was in that part of the house. Her eyes lingered on her father's orchid collection. She hoped she'd be able to keep it alive. Otherwise, her father might come back to haunt her. Her mind returned to Barnabas.

Where could he have gone? Perhaps his wife can shed some light on his utterly bizarre behavior. That's no way for him to act, even if I can't fire him.

"Angelique?" Marianne started back toward the living room.

The doorbell rang and the door creaked open.

"Trick or treat!"

"Oh, my! What a terrifying group of monsters! Don't eat me—take this candy instead," Angelique replied.

A chorus of "Thank you, ma'am" erupted from the children before they giggled and hurried away to the next house.

"Angelique?"

The housekeeper closed the door. "Yes, ma'am?"

"What on earth is wrong with your husband?"

"Beg pardon?"

"I realize we aren't friends, exactly, but you've worked for my father for some time. And now you're working for me. I saw Barnabas in the hallway, and he completely ignored me. That's unacceptable."

"You saw Barnabas? Are you sure?"

"Of course, I'm sure. Who else would be in the house?"

Surely Collins would have noticed if someone had broken in and was sneaking around.

The doorbell rang again and Angelique passed out more candy.

"Will you be wanting dinner, ma'am?"

A door slammed somewhere in the house.

"No. Jeremy and I stopped for dinner on the way home. I'd really like to speak with Barnabas in the morning."

"Yes, ma'am."

Jeremy and Collins came in from the kitchen, and they all headed up the stairs together. The dog made himself comfortable in his bed with a half-chewed rawhide bone. Jeremy unbuttoned his shirt, then turned on the water in the jacuzzi tub.

The pipes hissed, then a blurt of muddy water splashed into the tub. The stream of rusty liquid got thicker, then quit.

Marianne sighed. "Guess Daddy didn't use it any time recently."

Jeremy closed the tap and rubbed her shoulder. "S'alright. We'll get an even better one."

"We still have the champagne."

He reached for the bottle. "Except I forgot the glasses."

"At this point, we may as well have it by the fireplace in the kitchen, since we're going down there anyway."

Collins followed them down the stairs. Marianne smiled as Angelique pretended to cower in fear at a collection of vampires and pirates standing in the open doorway.

"She does a great job. Don't think we could run the house without her."

Jeremy glanced over his shoulder at the housekeeper. "Yes, but what about the butler?"

"I suppose we didn't need much buttling when we've been here in past Christmases."

She retrieved some champagne flutes while Jeremy pushed the button beside the hearth. A gas-fueled flame danced around realistic ceramic logs.

Cassandra was muttering under her cover. Marianne moved closer so she could hear what the bird said.

"You're hurting me! Stop it. Stop it!"

Her voice changed to a lower pitch. "I'm gonna kill you. I've had enough. Today is the day you're gonna kick it."

Back to higher pitch. "No! Barnabas, please!"

Marianne jumped when the champagne cork popped out of the bottle.

Cassandra let out a blood-curdling scream. "Watch out! Watch out!" Then the parrot spoke in a trembling voice. "What did you do? Now what? Now what, Jim?" The bird made a sad trill. "I don't know. Game room."

Marianne looked up to see Angelique standing in the doorway. Tears streamed down her face.

"Angelique? What's the matter?"

Jeremy guided the tearful woman to the table and pulled out a chair for her. "Your father saved my life, ma'am. Barnabas had been at the wet bar again. He was a mean drunk, you know. He took one of the knives out of the block and grabbed my arm. Said he was gonna kill me. Jim—your father—came in and shot him."

"What?" Marianne covered her mouth.

"Barnabas was dead. Probably before he hit the ground. I didn't know what to do. Jim dragged him to the game room and I helped him put Barnabas in the freezer."

Jeremy's face contorted. "You mean the one for all the ice cream…?"

"Yes."

"Then what did you do?"

"He's still in there. That's when Jim had his heart attack. I called 911 for him. Barnabas was the last thing on my mind. Now what?"

Marianne surveyed the back yard. There was still a lot of work to do, but the pool was sparkling clean, and the weeds had been cleared. She and Jeremy walked up the paving to the tennis court.

The old court had been jackhammered up—it was too damaged to repair. They'd put in a new one, this was their maiden game on the new concrete.

"You don't suppose they'll look too hard for him, do you?" Jeremy ran his hand across the net.

"Doubt it. If they think he disappeared voluntarily…" Marianne shrugged.

Jeremy put his hands on his lower back and stretched. "My back is still sore from all that digging."

Marianne tapped the court with her racquet. "At least he's not in the freezer anymore."

"Yeah. I hated throwing out all that ice cream. Your dad always got the good stuff. Glad Angelique knew exactly what to get to restock it."

Through the French doors, Marianne watched the housekeeper working in the kitchen. "Yes. Good help is hard to find."

TRUE CRIME CLUB

By Artemis Greenleaf

WELCOME to our virtual meeting for the Houston chapter of the True Crime Society. It's Tuesday night live!" Elizabeth smiled at the screen, and stacks of electronic boxes filled with people, smiled back. So far, twenty-seven people had joined.

"We'll just wait a few minutes before we get started to make sure any stragglers have a chance to get signed in. How's everybody been this week?"

A woman in a bright yellow shirt began mouthing words, but there was no sound.

"Susan, you're muted, hon."

Susan squinted at her screen for a moment. "Can you hear me now?"

"Yes, ma'am."

"I just wanted to let everybody know that I'm spending my lunch hour walking in the park. It's like a mini vacation, you know, to get out of the house and just have a change of scenery. And guess what? I've lost five pounds!"

Other members clapped, and there were responses of "Way to go!" "Good for you!"

"Oh, oh, oh!" A young woman with a green China doll haircut and bee sting lips waved her hand. "My uncle got out of the hospital. Nobody thought he was going to make it."

"Oh, that's excellent news, Leslie." Elizabeth smiled and nodded.

A name appeared in the waiting room. Alex Ridgeway. *That's the guy that signed up yesterday afternoon.* She clicked the button and admitted him to the call.

A woman with long dark hair appeared in a new box.

Oops! Guess it's an Alexandra, not an Alexander. "Welcome, Alex. This is our newest member. She joined online yesterday after watching the video on our Insta. Thank you, Patricia, for making that."

Patricia grinned. "I had a blast doing it."

Elizabeth shifted her microphone. "Alex, would you like to tell us a little bit about yourself, then we'll get started with our speaker." *Is that barbeque sauce on your cheek? You should always do a mirror check before you turn the camera on.*

A faint yowl and a thump came from somewhere. Alex looked over her shoulder, then turned back to face the camera. "The cat's knocked something over. I was just really curious about the group, so I thought I'd log in and check it out. Killers are fascinating. So, yeah… here I am."

Alex looked over her shoulder again, then reached up and adjusted her webcam so that it was focused more on her chin and decolletage.

Elizabeth cringed. *Can she not see her feed?* "Alright, then. Without further ado, I'd like to welcome Agent Samuel Berkowitz from the FBI. He's with the Behavioral Analysis Unit in Quantico, and he specializes in counter-terrorism. His latest book, *Free Radical,* is about how people get lured into violent organizations, and how to get them back out again. Alright, Sam, take it away."

"Good evening. I'd like to thank Elizabeth DeSalvo for that great introduction—she made me sound really good. Hope I don't disappoint. We're all here together tonight due to the miracle of the internet. Amazing thing, the World Wide Web. Don't you all agree?"

The people who had their cameras on nodded.

"Now, despite its many charms, the web has a dark side. You don't know who's really lurking on the other side of your screen."

The bang of a slamming door made everyone jump.

Elizabeth broke in, "I'm just going to put everyone on mute. Sorry. I should have done that earlier."

She glanced at Alex, who was watching something over her shoulder.

"Now, as I was saying," Agent Berkowitz started.

A young, sandy-haired man appeared in the hallway over Alex's shoulder. Elizabeth sighed with relief. At least there was someone there with her. Elizabeth had been getting concerned, as the new member had seemed very distracted by noises going on behind her.

Alex swiveled completely around to face the man. He charged at her, rage distorting his face. She just sat there, arms in front as if she were holding something in her lap.

Elizabeth fumbled for her mouse. It took her three tries to click the "Unmute All" button.

"Alex! Alex, run!"

She stood up just as the man reached her. The webcam got knocked over, and there was only a view of a laptop keyboard.

The crack of a gunshot ripped through Elizabeth's headphones, followed closely by a guttural scream. *Oh. My. God.* "Alex! Alex!"

Her rectangle disappeared as her connection dropped.

"Elizabeth!" Berkowitz shouted. "Call 9-1-1. Do it now."

She almost dropped her phone twice, her hands were shaking so badly.

"9-1-1. What's your emergency?"

The phone connected to the computer by Bluetooth, causing an echo as the conversation played out over the video conference.

"She's been shot." Elizabeth's voice was so high and thin she didn't recognize herself.

"Who's been shot?"

"A-a-alex. We were on a virtual meeting. This man just walked in and shot her. We all saw it."

"What's the address ma'am?"

"I. I don't know. It's all virtual. She was new…"

"Do you have a membership database?" Berkowitz asked.

"Yes. Of course! Aileen? Are you still-"

"I'm here! Hold on a sec…" Her fingers tapped furiously on the keyboard. "Got it! Alex Ridgeway, 2001 Green River Road, #1130."

Elizabeth repeated it to the dispatcher.

"Thank you, ma'am. Emergency services are on the way. Are you able to see the victim?"

"No. She disconnected."

"I see. Can you describe what happened?"

Elizabeth told her what she'd seen. The little red circle in the upper right of her screen caught her eye. "The whole thing is recorded! It was for a webinar, but…"

"Excellent. I need your contact information. A detective may stop by later this evening."

Elizabeth looked at the wastebasket near her feet. She thought she might vomit. But she managed to give the 9-1-1 operator her details.

Some of the True Crime Society members had signed off, but most were still on. Including Agent Berkowitz. This was the closest most of them had been to a true crime. Elizabeth just wanted to crawl into bed and hide under her covers.

"Okay, then," Agent Berkowitz said. "I think we'd better save this talk for another time. Is everyone okay?"

Elizabeth could see his eyes scanning the screen full of pale faces. She wasn't so sure she could answer 'yes' to his question.

"It's normal to be shaken up," Berkowitz said, looking at each individual frame. "Your body has a strong reaction to violence, because, well, *you* could be next. If your hands are shaking, you feel nausea, and your breathing is shallow, that's the adrenalin that flooded through your body when the flight-or-fight reaction kicked in. It'll pass as the excess adrenalin leaves your system, but it can't hurt to talk to someone about it—seeing violence first-hand like that can affect the witness almost as much as the victim."

"Thank you, Agent Berkowitz. I will, um, contact you later in the week."

"Certainly. When you give the police everyone's contact information, make sure they know I'm an FBI agent. I'm more than happy to assist with the case, if they would like."

"I'll do that."

Berkowitz dropped off the call.

"Alright, everybody. Stay safe. Go hug your loved ones. We'll reconvene next week. Good night."

Elizabeth shut down the call, then got up to make herself a cup of hot tea. She sat on her couch, covered with an afghan, sipping the hot drink and staring out the sliding glass door to the backyard.

It didn't help. It took another four hours for her to finally feel like she was winding down. She'd just stood up to get ready for bed when the doorbell rang. Elizabeth padded softly on bare feet to peer through the peephole. Two dark-haired men in suits stood there.

"Who is it?"

"Police, ma'am. Detectives Lucas and Rader."

"Hold your ID up to the peephole." She was half expecting them, but she was still spooked at the thought of strangers at her door.

They held them up, but between the dim porch light and the fish-eye distortion, Elizabeth couldn't tell if they were real or fake. But neither looked like the killer. "What do you want?"

"We just need to ask you some questions about the Alex Ridgeway incident."

They must be real if they know the details. Elizabeth flung open the door. "Come in, come in."

She led them to the living room. "Can I offer you anything to drink?"

The one that she thought was Rader said, "No, thank you."

"So, how can I help you?"

"The dispatcher said you might have a recording of the incident," Lucas replied.

"Yes." Elizabeth moved to the desk in the far corner and woke the laptop. Once she found the recording of the virtual meeting, she clicked on it and said, "I don't want to watch this again. I'll go in the kitchen and get myself some water."

Rader nodded, his eyes softening. "Yes ma'am. I think that's a great idea."

When Elizabeth heard the gunshot, she drank most of the water and had to refill her glass.

"Ma'am?" Detective Lucas called. "Could you send this to me?"

Elizabeth came back into the living room. "Of course. Do you have a card with your email on it?"

"Yes." He reached into his pocket and drew out a fancy metal business card case. Mother of pearl gleamed on the inside as he opened it.

Elizabeth sat back down at her computer. "I'll load it up to the cloud, then send you a link. I think it's too big to email."

"If you could get a list of all the attendees and their contact information, that'd be helpful."

"Already downloaded." She started to upload the video.

"So you've never actually met Alex Ridgeway, is that correct?" Lucas asked.

"Yes, that's correct. Is Alex okay?" Elizabeth suspected she already knew the answer.

Detective Rader shook his head. "No, ma'am. I'm sorry. If it's any comfort, the cat will be okay, though."

"Cat?"

"Ridgeway's cat. Yes. It came through the surgery just fine."

Elizabeth's hand flew to her mouth. "What happened to it?"

"The intruder stabbed it, but lucky for the cat, missed any vital organs."

"How awful. As I said before, I didn't really know Alex, but she seemed nice."

The detectives looked at each other. Lucas pulled out his cell phone and scrolled around on it for a moment. He showed her a photo of a young man. Sandy blond hair. Blue eyes.

Elizabeth leaned back. "That's the killer."

Detective Lucas shook his head. "No, ma'am. That's Alex Ridgeway."

TRUNKS

By Holly Dey

WHO did your ink?" The guy in the tank top had a man-bun and one of his arms was covered from knuckles to shoulder in tattoos.

"Pug. He died a few years ago."

He stepped closer and peered at my arm like he was sizing up an item at a garage sale. "Nice. Dude. Pug was a legend." He waved and continued down the sidewalk.

I rubbed my upper arm. After all this time, the bejeweled elephant still raised her trunk proudly. It was late October, almost Halloween. I shuddered.

I once ran off to join the circus. It was, I don't know…twenty years ago? My kids were grown and my wife had been taking private lessons with the tennis pro at the country club for a while. I didn't think she'd even notice I was gone.

I had found an ad for an assistant elephant keeper for a circus that's headquartered about a hundred miles away in Dante, Florida. Training provided during the winter, then travel May through October. I'd even found a set of vintage nesting steamer trunks for my stuff. Maybe not the most efficient, but I love old things.

The Ninth Circle Circus always held performances in their hometown the last week of October. Halloween Homecoming, they called it. I arrived two days before the troupe and I unloaded my stack of impractical trunks in one of the tiny houses onsite provided to employees. It would have been easier to have just gotten an extra-large suitcase, I suppose. But the three of them grouped together, in all their old-fashioned glory, had made this feel like a real adventure.

I spent the majority of my time exploring Dante, the surrounding small town that was mostly populated by retired circus performers. There were all the shops you'd expect, and then some. But there was only one that I felt compelled to visit.

Perched on the slate roof of Orpheus's Oddities was an eight-foot plastic lyre that had seen better days. There were a few patches of gold paint on the oversized instrument, but it was mostly a swampy grey. I wasn't sure if that was by design or just entropy.

Wind chimes tinkled when I opened the door. I saw no one in the shop—the cashier must be in the back and would probably turn up in a minute. Casually posed mannequins stood all around the shop, dressed in sparkling circus costumes and antique jewelry. A trapeze hung from the ceiling and a life-size acrobat hung by his knees from the bar, forever ready to catch a non-existent flyer.

A taxidermied white horse stood close to the door, three of its hooves fixed to a heavy stand, while the fourth was raised in an elegant arc. Hot pink, glitter-sprinkled feathers to rival a Vegas showgirl rose behind its ears and another, even larger bouquet adorned its back, held on by a leather strap that encircled its middle. The brown glass eyes that stared at me from its majestic head were so realistic I found it… off-putting. I hurried past it into the heart of the shop.

A statue stopped me cold. On the glass counter, a life-sized contortionist squatted, her back bent at such an extreme angle that her placid face looked out from between her feet. It made me think of a spider, even though she had only half the limbs of an arachnid. A beam of afternoon sunlight cut through the dingy window above the wooden door and highlighted her face. The vertical slit of a pupil in her yellow eyes didn't make me feel any more at ease.

"Anything I can help you find?"

Ahh! I almost jumped out of my skin when the contortionist spoke to me. She began unbending herself.

"No. No, thank you. I was just looking. Got a job at the circus and moved in yesterday."

"Oh." She grinned at me. Her eyes were an ordinary brown now. Must have been a trick of the light that created that creepy effect. "You must be Terry Gillespie. I heard they hired a new pooper scooper."

"Yeah. That's me. Hope there's more to the job than that, though." I hadn't really thought about what duties an assistant elephant keeper would be performing before I applied for the job.

"My brother's the elephant boss. Circus owns three of them— Ellie, Peanut, and Queenie. They're all really sweet. Queenie's the mom and Ellie and Peanut are her daughters." The way her eyes flicked up to the ceiling when she said 'brother' made me wonder about their relationship.

"Is there a dad elephant?"

"Rorschach, but he passed away a few years ago."

"Oh. Sorry to hear that."

Her smile showed too many teeth. "If you have any questions while you're looking around, just ask."

I nodded and continued with my perusal. The store wasn't the standard box from a strip mall. The building had clearly been someone's house once upon a time. I guessed this had been the living room, or possibly parlor, depending on how old the house was.

My eyes fell on a shelf of preserved mutations. A tiny, two-headed pig floated in a jar of formaldehyde. A frog with four extra legs, placed randomly on its body, stared out from a brick of acrylic. A stuffed kitten with a single enormous eye, eight legs, and two tails sent a shiver down my backbone. A Fiji mermaid sat next to that, the clumsy surgery that grafted a monkey head and torso onto a fish's tail painfully obvious.

I moved to the next room. Bigfoot print castings, a clump of alleged Yeti hair, and blurry blowups of UFOs lined one wall. A gallery of photos and paintings of sideshow freaks took up the other three. I kind of liked the impressionist take on the bearded lady.

Four additional rooms held circus memorabilia, old costume jewelry, and circus-themed home décor and souvenirs. I thought about getting a big top shower curtain for my daughter—she loves that kind of thing.

A glass cabinet in the souvenir room contained pewter figurines. Ringmaster. Clown. Lion. Elephants in several poses. One elephant, its trunk raised proudly, stood out from the rest. It was the only one of its kind, probably the last on the shelf, because it was so much better than the others. Purple and pink crystals—I assumed they were rhinestones—sparkled in the headdress beneath fluffy plumes of purple feathers. I had to get it, given my new job.

I set the statuette on the counter by the cash register. "There's no price on this one."

"All the figurines are the same price." A sly smile edged up the corners of her lips.

Seemed reasonable. I wasn't in the mood to haggle, anyway.

She rang up the statuette. "They say a raised trunk is for good luck." She grabbed the elephant with a wad of tissue paper and shoved it into a bag.

"Thanks. I'll need all the luck I can get."

"Yes. You very well might." She grinned her stomach-churning grin.

I took my purchase and left, not sure I ever wanted to set foot in that store again. I could order a shower curtain online for Genie.

When I got back to my tiny house on the circus property, I unwrapped the elephant and set her on the windowsill in my bedroom. Purple and pink blobs splotched the white paint of the sill where sunlight touched the jewels. The elephant just looked happy, and it made me feel happy looking at her. Don't know how I knew it was a her, but I knew.

I was supposed to be at work at 8:00 AM, so I left my house at 7:45. I'd found the elephant enclosure when I first arrived, but I wasn't entirely sure where in the oversized building I was meeting my new supervisor. As I got closer, I saw the grey forms of three elephants in the reinforced pen. But no people.

A woman in tights and a sports bra was heading in my direction.

"Excuse me? Miss? I'm looking for Elliot Spencer. Can you tell me where to find him?"

Her eyes boldly scanned my body from head to toe and back up again. "You must be the new bullhand. You're a *lot* better looking than the last two. Shame."

Last two? Is there a high turnover rate? "Um… thanks?"

She pointed to a towering barn. "You'll probably find Spence in his office in there."

"Thank you."

I'd seen tall elephant and giraffe barns on trips to the zoo when the kids were little. But this one seemed less airy and bright. Dark, heavy timbers supported the tall awning, which cast the entryway in deep shadow.

It's not like I need *this job*, I reminded myself, not sure where the resistance to entering the elephant barn was coming from. My footsteps echoed off the concrete walkway and were swallowed by the gloom.

"Hello?" I called.

There was no answer.

Further down the hall, I spotted a lighted office window, so I hurried toward it. *Should I knock, or just go in? He is expecting me.* I knocked on the door before opening it. A man a little older than me looked up, a phone receiver clamped to his face.

I looked around while he finished up his call.

"You Gillespie?"

"That's me."

"Fleur said you were in the shop yesterday."

"Your sister?"

His lips pursed slightly. "The one and only. Alright, let's get started."

He gave me a tour of the elephant facility and introduced me to the pachyderms. As it turned out, Fleur's description of the job as a pooper scooper wasn't that far off. I shoveled food at one end and manure at the other. The elephants were friendly, brushing me with their trunks when I was in the pen. I didn't mind, except when they got too personal. Peanut was bad about groping.

Halloween would fall on a Saturday this year. Spence told me they expected an especially large crowd. Dante wasn't that far from Jacksonville, so there were always plenty of big-city suckers, ready to lose their money on the midway during that glorious Halloween Homecoming week. I fell into the rhythm of life in the circus. My favorite part was watching the aerialists from backstage. Benders not so much. They made me queasy.

Circus life was hard work, harder than I'd expected. Didn't need to worry about going to the gym. I'd only been there a week and thought I was in decent shape, but I had to go up a notch on my belt to keep my pants from falling off.

It was closing in on three AM. I sat in Spence's office, and he poured us both a drink. The midway hadn't shut down until two to take advantage of the sizeable crowds. The Halloween Homecoming had been a runaway success. There was an afternoon matinee tomorrow, but for all intents and purposes, this season had ended with a bang.

Spence got up and stood near a picture of four elephants. I recognized Queenie, Peanut, and Ellie. Didn't know the fourth, but suspected it was Rorschach. I coughed after guzzling a little too much of the liquor. I wasn't entirely sure what it was. Spence had poured it from a crystal decanter, and I'd assumed it was whiskey, but I was wrong. It was not like anything I'd ever tasted, but I could pick out a few familiar flavors. Anise. Honey. Vinegar.

My head drooped against my chest. My normal bedtime was about five hours ago. Spence was talking. His words meant something, but I was too tired to understand what. I'd figure it out in the morning.

"C'mon." Spence opened the door.

I stumbled after him, even less coordinated than I expected.

Queenie, Ellie, and Peanut stood in their stalls, stuffing hay into their mouths. Well, Ellie and Peanut were. Queenie stood quietly, facing us.

I leaned against the bars to hold myself up. "I should probably hit the sack. I'm beat."

"In a minute. I want you to see something."

"It can't wait until morning?"

He had the same unpleasant expression his sister did—a grimace that was more snarl than smile. It made my skin crawl.

Something touched my hair and I jumped. It was Queenie, stroking my head with her trunk. "Well? What do you want to show me?"

Spence whistled an unfamiliar tune.

Queenie's trunk shot out like a snake and pulled me hard against the bars. Something else wrapped around my right leg, then my left arm. I looked down to see two more elephant trunks. Another one grabbed my left leg.

Wait. Four? "Queenie!" I grunted. "Let go!" She ignored me. "Spence?"

He stood there in the darkness. "Sorry, Terry."

The elephant tugged harder, as if she was trying to pull me through the bars. My ribs ached, like they would crack at any moment. I gasped for air. Instinctively, I lowered my head and bit down as hard as I could on the tender tip of Queenie's trunk, clamping down until she released me, bellowing in pain.

I staggered away from the bars, out of reach. I don't know what that thing was that stood behind the bars, but it wasn't the Queenie I knew. Six trunks flailed like angry snakes in front of her face. Her head had widened and a third eye, smoldering red like the other two, had appeared in the middle of her forehead.

Teeth—not elephant teeth, but knife-blade piranha teeth— glistened in the slime that oozed from her mouth. My head swam. I tried to shake it off as I bolted for the door. Spence stuck out a boot and tripped me. I sprawled on the concrete, busting my lip and skinning my knee, but somehow I was back on my feet and running in an instant. I raced to my tiny house, locked the door, and hid under the bed.

What was in that drink? LSD? I forced myself to take deep breaths. *Calm down, Terry. You're so tired you're hallucinating.*

Feet crunched on the gravel path outside the house. *No. No, no, no, no.*

"Teeeerry. I know you're in there. I can smell you. Come on out." Spence sounded like he was trying to coax a lost kitten out of a tree.

This isn't happening. None of this is real. But I didn't move from my hiding place.

Glass shattered in the front room. The front door opened, and heavy footsteps crunched on the remains of the window.

"Teeeeerry. Come out, come out wherever you are."

I held my breath, feeling like I was going to lose my lunch at any second. The house had only two rooms: a living room with a kitchenette and a bedroom. If I wasn't in the front room…

Spence whistled as he strolled through my house. That same weird tune from earlier. In the gap between the bedspread and the floor, I could see black boots, each footfall on the wood floor like a sledgehammer blow.

The boots stopped right in front of my face at the end of the bed. "Bingo."

The double window above the bed shattered, and glass rained on the floor. Suddenly, the bed was picked up and tossed onto its side.

Six trunks had swarmed in from the broken window, searching for me. I wasn't sure I was out of reach.

Spence shook his head. "You're making this so much harder than it has to be, Terry."

I scooted backward, slicing my palm on a shard of window. A trunk stretched toward my head, getting longer as I retreated until I hit the wall. It found my foot and dragged me toward the gaping hole where the window used to be. I clawed at the area rug, but only succeeded in bringing it with me.

The elephant figurine had been knocked to the floor and lay in the window debris. It wasn't much of a weapon, but it was the only one I had. I grabbed the statuette, and it almost slipped out of my blood-slicked hand. But I held on and bashed the trunk that was tugging me up through the ruined window.

There was a sizzle, and I almost gagged on the acrid smell of burning flesh. Queenie screamed, dropping me onto the wood floor. Before I could get up, the other five trunks wrapped around my arms and legs, and I thought my shoulder was going to dislocate as she tugged and shook my arm, trying to make me drop the pewter elephant.

I don't know how I held on to it. Maybe because the drying blood had become sticky.

Queenie squeezed my arm so tightly I started losing feeling in it. If I dropped the figurine, that would be the end of me.

I struggled, trying to turn my body and break her hold. She shook me and I felt like a mouse in the jaws of a cat. I wasn't going to fit through that broken window. Not in one piece, anyway. Jagged glass studded the frame. I kicked my legs, trying to maneuver one of her trunks onto a sharp edge. No luck.

The monstrous elephant pulled me against the window frame. My body was being crushed against the center bar and I fought for air. As my body contorted, I heard a pop. I hoped it was the wood and not my spine. My arm slid toward my thigh.

The figurine brushed one of Queenie's trunks.

She bellowed, and her grip loosened.

I smashed the statuette into her other trunks, burning them, too. She let go and jerked them from the window, dropping me into the broken glass. As I struggled for breath, I heard her thudding footsteps retreat into the darkness.

"What did you do?" Spence growled.

I whirled on him. His eyes were reptilian. Gold with vertical pupils. I almost dropped the statuette.

"Where did you get that?" he snarled as he backed away from me.

"At Orpheus."

"No, you didn't. We'd never carry something like that." Then he growled, a low rumble deep in his chest. "Fleur," he muttered just loud enough for me to hear before fleeing out the door.

I huddled in my closet until dawn, pewter elephant clutched in my hand. As soon as the sun bobbed above the horizon, I threw my few possessions into my steamer trunks and hit the road, with no idea where I was going, just wanting to put as much distance as possible between me and Dante, Florida. I got on I-10 and headed west.

Two days later, I was at the edge of a town whose name I can't remember, sitting in a twenty-four-hour diner having stale coffee and a questionable piece of cherry pie. This had turned out to be a whole lot more adventure than I'd bargained for. Maybe what I really needed was a place in a small town. Just an anonymous retiree with a little house I could lock and leave when I wanted to travel. There'd have to be some things to do in the area, of course. But an out of the way place, a friendly backwater where a circus was not likely to visit. I'd had enough circus excitement for the next three lifetimes.

I hadn't been paying much attention to the TV that hung above the end of the counter, but a video of a fire caught my eye. The volume was off, but I read the chyron.

"Overnight, the winter quarters of the Ninth Circle Circus burned to the ground. The compound housed a circus troupe during the off season, and the small town of Dante had built up around it." The video switched to a still of a young woman, face smeared in soot. I almost choked on my cold coffee. It was Fleur, the contortionist. "Tragically, firefighters have only been able to rescue a single resident. Cadaver dogs have been called in, but no bodies have been recovered as of yet."

I didn't know what had happened. Had Fleur torched the camp? Or had they left her behind in the flames? Heck, maybe Queenie was so furious about being denied her…sacrifice that she lit it up. Either way, I needed to put more space between me and Dante. If it weren't for the nasty cut on my hand, I would have chalked the whole thing up to a doctored drink. But that raised its own questions. I didn't think there was a reason for them to come after me, but then again, I didn't think I was going to get attacked by some perversion of an elephant, either.

I pushed away my half-eaten pie. Grabbing my check and heading to the door, I rubbed the bejeweled elephant in my pocket like a worry stone.

An extra dose of luck never hurt anybody.

If you enjoyed this book, please consider leaving a review at your favorite book site. Reviews help other readers find and enjoy new books!

To explore more content from Artemis Greenleaf, A.B. Richards, and Holly Dey, please visit BlackMareBooks.com

For more content from Claire Murray, please visit cam-writes.com